About the Author

Eugene Tossany is the chosen pen name of a U.S. author who started her editorial journey in third grade. After pursuing life and achieving accolades, awards and an Army Commendation Medal, Eugene picked up the pen again, in 2019. After the birth of her Down Syndrome daughter and after living in Israel, she crafted an inspirational manuscript, citing experiences, ancient research and wisdom, as well as a creative perspective from her indirect Literary Mentor, Stephen King.

The Down Syndrome Superhero

Eugene Tossany

The Down Syndrome Superhero

Olympia Publishers
London

www.olympiapublishers.com
OLYMPIA PAPERBACK EDITION

A CIP catalogue record for this title is
available from the British Library.

ISBN: 978-1-78830-779-6

First Published in 2020

Olympia Publishers
Tallis House
2 Tallis Street
London
EC4Y 0AB

Printed in Great Britain

Dedication

Dedicated to a Trisomy 21 Angel, Charlie, and our faithful canine companion, Zeke.

Acknowledgements

I would like to acknowledge all the support and efforts from family, friends, medical personnel, therapists, care providers, attorneys and all the loving families who teach their children inclusivity of persons with special needs.

Prologue

Dear Parent(s) and/or Guardians,

This is a sensitive book that deals with what was once considered adult topics. However, our children are increasingly exposed to more sensitive themes via social media. And we, as parents and/or guardians, must ask ourselves the tough questions. At what age should I speak with my child about sexual intercourse? Is it too early for them to understand how to protect themselves from pedophiles? How do I explain rape, in a way that makes sense and doesn't emotionally damage my child's innocence?

My daughter is a Down Syndrome child and one of many who faces societal challenges. But her strength and resolve have shown me the beautiful resilience within each of us. At some point, I too will have the ever-important conversation about 'the birds and the bees,' but in a much more meaningful way. Her ability to understand the difference between right and wrong behaviors is affected by the developmental delays associated with Down's. Therefore, my conversation should and will be structured to include the full scope of sexuality: from the sanctity of choice to the debilitation of perversion.

Having these types of conversations is my form of preventative protection, rather than defensive protection. My special needs child, as well as other special needs children, should be armed with knowledge, wisdom, and understanding. If a predator intimidates my child, I want her reaction to mirror everything she has been taught:

1. Listen to intuition
2. Identify a bad situation
3. Evaluate options
4. Find Safety
5. Communicate

That first gut reaction can be the difference between life and death or harm. Too often, we ignore those internal alarms. Especially, if it is somebody we know or feel comfortable with, perhaps within our own families. A child should know that his/her intuition takes precedence over familial relationships.

Identifying a bad situation would be akin to acknowledging negative intuition and accepting there could be a bad situation unfolding. This would be the second step after listening to our gut feeling. Sometimes this stage can cause anxiety, as though our mind is prepping our body for an appropriate response.

Evaluating the options would include, but are not limited to, looking around for a cell phone, an exit, an objective adult (someone not associated with the offending party), a whistle, or a place to hide. Although we learn about the fight or flight response at an early age, not many of us are taught what to do with that initial response for action.

Finding safety is the next step, after evaluating what kind of situation is presenting itself. It could be a combination of acting on any one of the numerous options. For example, blowing a whistle and then running to the nearest adult. If handicapped, blowing a whistle, making lots of noise, and staying put until the danger passes. The exception would be if the child needs to move themselves from an isolated area to an open area, where attackers might be reticent to confront a potential victim.

Communication is the final step and involves notifying the proper authorities, and speaking truthfully. If a child has a cell phone or is near a phone, 911 is the first method. A child should not feel embarrassed or as though their experience does not matter. As a parent, I must listen to what my child is telling me and not overreact. Children should be children and not have to constantly arm themselves with appropriate responses.

I am a huge proponent of clear communication and preventative protection. Although the harshness of sexual predators is only detailed within one chapter of this book, the content could be considered shocking for a young reader. It is up to the parent or guardian's discretion to have certain conversations before your child reads the book, while reading the book, after reading the book, or not at all.

Either way, the surrounding chapters are filled with themes sure to support an active imagination and literary adventure.

Respectfully,
Ms. Eugene Tossany

Chapter 1

I put the oranges in a neat row, under the shiny lamp that looks like a spaceship. The lamp was a gift from Nana, and it reflected objects around it. It was a silver lamp, but the flecks of dust made it look grey, like a moth. The lamp's hood reminded me of a large fabric hat – a textured veil of glowing sunlight.

I walked into the room for a reason and with a purpose. Decorating oranges is a favorite craft project, which would explain why my room was covered with glitter and fuzzy, miniature pom-poms. As I was watching the neighbors' dogs run around the yard, I decided I would glue a tail to a Valencia. Instead of felt piping, I thought I would use a feather from one of the dusters. Mom would like to know that the dusters were being used for something, other than the intended lamp cleaning.

I knelt on all fours and scoured the carpet, searching for the duster and my bottle of Gorilla glue. Zeke, our family's cuddly Shih Tzu, greeted me with a wet kiss on the tip of my ear. He is eight years old, but an old man in dog years. I giggled and puckered my lips to make a kissing sound, just as he was leaning in for a smooch. The result was a tongue tickle at the corner of my mouth. I giggled again and tugged at his ear to show my appreciation.

Aha! I saw the Gorilla glue wedged between a shoe and a roll of paper towels. As I was reaching for the glue, I noticed the lower part of the wall reflecting a silver light. With the glue in hand, I crawled backward and glanced up at the nightstand. The moon rock was shining its familiar halo, alerting me to a portal opening. The feather project would have to wait.

Chapter 2

The day I found the moon rock there was a great deal of thunder and sparks of electricity in the air. I had been outside, exploring our backyard, and following a trail of leaves. Rolling hills were leading to a cleared path, where a central dog park was surrounded with neighboring houses. Zeke was with me, tugging at his leash, anxious because of the crackle of the energized atmosphere.

I remember a long wooden fence, sectioning off a development area. There were hundreds of trees and lightning bugs. There was a small grid where the tulips met the corner of the fence and long grass caressed the beams. Tucked underneath the grass was a strong glow of silver light. It was not much bigger than the palm of my hand. There was no trespass warning sign, and the gate was hinged with a small hook. Zeke and I gave each other a nod, as though we knew a shared adventure would be just the logical next step.

I put my hand on the gate, unhooked the latch, and pushed past the large, swooping tree branches. Zeke sprinted around some shrubs and headed straight for the shining patch of grass. I pulled on his leash, like a rein, to make sure he did not get too far ahead of me. As I walked near the object, I felt a slight drizzle of rain and a magnetic ripple of an air current. All of a sudden, the rain bent into a rainbow above what could only be described as a large grey rock, with a bright central core and swirling sparkles. The miniature rainbow was absorbing the sparks from the grey rock. I could feel my eyes watering as I stared at the projection of what looked like a window to a parallel galaxy. Zeke could sense there was magic in the air. He whined and clawed at the grass around the rock.

From above, the sky seemed to open up and what looked like a muscular arm reached down and zapped the rock. The flecks of burgundy and turquoise light bounced from the sides of the rock and illuminated the grass. The entire area, where we were standing, seemed as though we stepped into a time warp. Everything around us was still: the butterflies, crickets, and birds. The rock soared up to eye level and danced mid-air. The central green core shone with a brilliance that could only be described as galactic. The sparkles looked like a star pattern from actual galaxies.

As I was mesmerized by the rock, I saw the thin arms of its star patterns seep into the air. The glitter kept expanding and Zeke barked and hid between my feet. I felt my blood pressure rise, and I could hear my heart thumping, as a jolt of light touched the tips of my hair. I screamed and Zeke barked, with surprise! I wasn't sure what was happening, so I jumped back and pulled on Zeke's leash. My scalp felt really tingly, and there was an odd sensation, like an egg yolk spilling down the sides of my head.

For a moment, I thought I was dead. Zeke barked, and I could tell the tingle was making its way through his little body. He sneezed once and then started rubbing his face with his paw. What was happening? The environment was so surreal that I didn't want to interrupt it with screams of help. Instead, I reached down and picked up the grey rock.

All kinds of weirdness were coming from the rock. Its brilliant light changed from silver to purple, and the green core was subdued. The swirls of sparkle and glitter were fading, as the purple color became more pronounced. Then, the rock spoke, but not in a voice. It sounded like a dialogue bubble floating past my ear. The thunder was still roaring, and all I could understand was a phrase that sounded like 'HELP HER.' Zeke heard it, too. His head cocked to the side, and he sniffed the air, as though he could smell the passing phrase.

Overcoming fear, I put the grey rock in my pocket and decided I would take it home, where it could be further examined. Somehow, standing in the middle of a gated land lot holding a glowing rock seemed a little dangerous. I saw too many science fiction movies, where kids could be pulled into alternate dimensions and figured I wouldn't take my chances.

I tugged at Zeke's leash, then turned to the fenced entrance. Zeke was probably thinking the same as me, because he bolted, with me still holding the leash. Zeke was already several steps ahead of me, so I let him lead my disbelieving self to the sidewalk. I wanted to jump up and down and let the neighborhood know what we had just seen, within a matter of minutes. As I looked around, I noticed the usual pattern of Saturday happenings: lawn mowing, car washing, yard sales, and bike riding. Were we the only ones who experienced the other side? I wasn't sure what the other side was, but it was definitely there and accessible from the abandoned lot.

When we arrived at the front door of our home, my mom breathed a sigh of relief. She was waiting at the window. "The surveillance system timed out. I wasn't sure if you were at the neighbor's house or if you were at the lot across the street." Her brow furrowed as she looked at my wet clothes. "What's that in your pocket?" she pointed at the bulge jutting from my thigh.

"A glowing rock that I found hidden in the grass." I released Zeke from his leash and turned to go upstairs.

"I'm interested. Can I see it?" she said with a playful smile.

"Yea, Mom. It was really cool. A rainbow formed above the rock, as it was raining and thundering." I did not tell her about the muscular arm, the galactic glow, or the invisible dialogue bubble because somehow, I knew she would not understand. I grabbed the rock from my pocket, breathed some hot air on the center part, and attempted to polish it with my shirt.

The rock stopped glowing, responding like a turtle and masking its inner swirls. My mom looked at it and responded, "Nice! I have no idea why you would want a grey rock." She squinted her eyes at me and asked, "Why is your hair filled with static? It's standing straight up."

Ignoring her question, I tossed the rock into the air and said, "What if it's a magic rock?"

"Then we would rub it and ask if it can bring us good fortune," she said. At the time, I was disappointed with her response. I felt like it was cliché to make fun of a teenager's imagination. Most of the kids my age were into booze, loud music, and Instagram. And here I was, infatuated with a mystical rock.

After a long pause, my mom sat up from the table and reached for her cell phone. Changing subjects, she said, "Let me call your dad and make sure he's still picking up dinner." I nodded and silently turned to exit the kitchen, taking my pride with me.

My mom held the cell phone to her ear and then shouted, "Oh, and throw a towel on Zeke! He's dripping everywhere." She maneuvered herself into the living room and left me to take care of Zeke and resume my Saturday activities, which usually consisted of art and watching old movies.

I bounded up the stairs, flung my shoes off, grabbed a T-shirt, and started drying Zeke. My room suddenly smelled of wet dog, so I grabbed a crafted orange and pushed my fingernail into the skin. The orange tang aroma was a welcome relief.

I threw the rock on the bed and was upset that it was dormant. Staring at the rock, I crawled into my bean bag chair and pulled up a blanket. I closed my eyes and tried to put myself back into the empty lot. There was so much that occurred in such a small amount of time. I was sure I should write it all down, so that I could revisit the details. Of all the interesting phenomenon, I was thinking about the muscular arm and the command to help 'HER.'

Speaking of the rock, where should I hide it? After glancing around the room, I decided I would put the rock inside a jewelry box. The little jewelry box was from Nana or grandma. We called her Nana instead of grandma because I was too young to pronounce grandma, and Nana kind of held.

It was a wooden jewelry box with stenciled flowers. The inside of the jewelry box was a vibrant melon felt color. The only piece of jewelry inside was a small pearl ring, bequeathed to me after Nana's death. I put the rock next to the ring and closed the jewelry box. I hid it inside my sock drawer, nestled between a hidden stash of payday candy bars. My mom probably knew about the hidden stash, but she hadn't said anything yet.

I glanced out the window, as I was closing the drawer and saw that it was still raining. I guess Zeke and I would have to stay inside. At the moment, Zeke was lying on the floor, with his chin resting on the side of the dog bed. He was snoring. His dog bed was large enough for the two of us to snuggle so, I curled up next to him, with a blanket, and thought about what we would be having for dinner.

Chapter 3

I could feel Zeke's heart beating alongside mine. His fur was still a little damp from the excursion, but his body felt very warm. I closed my eyes and could feel the wariness of my muscles, probably from being so tense when I was witnessing the magical rock scenario. For the first time, I wondered if it was a moon rock, or some kind of meteorite, from space. Those thoughts persisted as I drifted into a deep sleep.

My eyes opened and beheld a beautiful scenic view. Although my body felt heavy, I was moving with great ease. I stood up and walked to the middle of my room, where the air around me was fuzzy, as though somebody smudged the edges of the air particles. The walls were clear and seemed to be breathing.

From outside, a gentle rainbow appeared to shoot up from the ground at the room. First, the floor filled up with bright colors, and then sparkles led the way upward to an area near the ceiling. The color grew from the floor and reached the light fixture. I held up my finger and expected to see a red pulsing light, like the scene from the movie *E.T.* Instead, I noticed all of my skin was glowing with different colors. It felt like I was being energized with color.

While I was admiring the changing colors of my skin tone, a door slowly appeared in the wall opposite my desk. It was a basic white door, with a gold knob. Since the walls were clear and the door was white, it was the only object I was drawn to. I moved toward it and reached for the doorknob. I grabbed hold and turned it clockwise. The door opened without a sound. Beyond the doorway was a rainbow path leading to the sidewalk. I wasn't sure if the path continued past the neighbor's house, or if it stopped at a certain point in front of our large willow tree.

Zeke appeared at my side. He was much taller and fluffier than the real Zeke. He seemed happy to see me, so we stepped through the door together. He looked up at me and spoke. I laughed because his voice sounded like that of a child's. He said, "Hello, I can speak now." I gestured a thumbs up and smiled.

Once we were in the new dimension, the door closed, but I could still see the bedroom. Zeke ran ahead of me and then turned around and barked. He wanted me to follow him. I skipped past him and stayed on the rainbow path, which was wide enough for four people to walk across.

Unexpectedly, the path led to the empty lot, where Zeke and I had been that afternoon. The sky above the lot was dark, gloomy, and filled with storm clouds. As we walked closer, I noticed that I was looking down at a version of myself and Zeke, standing in the exact place where we were before. The rock started glowing its purple and silver colors. Just then, a strike of light stretched down to the ground and zapped the rock.

In the distance, I heard a scream and my attention shifted. Up the street, I saw a little girl running from a white van. The side of the van had its door open, and a large man was hanging from it and trying to grip the girl's coat. I started stomping my feet and yelled, "SOMEBODY PLEASE, HELP HER!" My voice seemed to echo throughout the yard. Zeke began barking, and I was getting ready to chase and stop the van. I squinted my eyes and could see the license plates clearly, as though they were just five feet in front of my face.

I looked down and saw the previous version of myself and Zeke leaving the lot. What I couldn't see was which direction the van was headed. They missed the little girl and only snatched her purple coat, as she zigzagged into a neighbor's backyard. The dream vision started turning fuzzy, and it was hard to make out where the little girl ended up. Every instinct was telling me that she made it to safety and that I needed to go back to the sanctity of my room.

"Zeke! Let's go!" I yelled.

Zeke responded with, "I saw a purple coat" then he trotted back up the path to our home. I followed behind him trying to make sense of the scene that we had just witnessed. Was this part of a dream, or were we seeing something happen in front of us?"

The door was gone, but the walls were still clear. Zeke instinctively knew how to walk through the wall and enter the bedroom. I followed him and felt my skin tingle as I walked past the wall and into my familiar space. The rainbow colors were starting to fade, and I felt incredibly tired. Somehow, it made sense to position ourselves in the dog bed, just as we were before entering the dream vision. Zeke jumped in and said, "Now I lay me down to sleep," which was similar to a prayer I said before bed every night. I petted Zeke's head and curled up next to him.

Some untold amount of time later, my eyes opened, and I sat up in Zeke's dog bed. I pinched myself to make sure this was the real dimension. The pinch hurt, and I was satisfied with where I was. Zeke also sat up and looked at me with reassuring eyes. I waited to see if he would speak and when he didn't, I touched the tip of his nose and told him he was my best friend.

I stood up and stretched, feeling the strain in my neck from sleeping at such crooked angles. There, on my desk, was my yellow cell phone. My mind raced with all kinds of possible scenarios, and the only one that made sense was to call the police. I didn't give much thought to how I would relay the supernatural information. All I could think about was intervening to save the life of a little girl. I grabbed the cell phone from the top of my desk and immediately dialed 911.

After two rings, the operator answered, "911. What's your emergency?"

I responded, "Yes. I would like to report a possible kidnapping. The license plate is 630 ZPE. Delaware registration. A white van with a large man inside. He was wearing a dark brown hoodie." I completed the description and told the operator I would ask my parents to drive me to the police station. As I ended the phone call, I remembered a detail from the dream. The color purple was missing from the rainbow path.

Chapter 4

I asked my parents if they could drive me to the police station. Of course, they demanded an explanation of what prompted the call. I summarized as best I could, trying to make it sound like a dream warning. At first, my parents were convinced that I was mixing science fiction with the real world. They did not understand that my dream was a glimpse into a different dimension, and I didn't know how to make them believe. Maybe because of the Down Syndrome, it seemed like I was constantly explaining my perception of reality. I was frustrated.

There was a knock at the front door. My dad stood up from the table and made his way to the foyer. Curious, I followed him and then stepped into the living room. He opened the door, and a loud confident voice boomed into the entryway, "Good evening, sir. My partner and I are canvassing the neighborhood and asking if anybody has seen a suspicious white van driving up and down these streets, since yesterday." From my perspective, my dad was visibly stunned and at a loss for words.

He thought about his next sentence and then said, "Well, my daughter had a dream that she saw a white van chasing a little girl with a purple coat. She spoke to one of your Emergency Operators, but I'm not sure if she told her it was a dream."

"Well, that would be quite the dream, since that's exactly what happened," the first officer said.

"May we come in?" asked the second officer.

My dad stepped back from the door. "Yes. Come on in, and we can speak in the living room."

The two officers obliged and entered our living room. They removed their hats and stood next to each other, casually glancing at their surroundings. My mother entered the room quietly.

The blonde-haired officer looked at my mom and dad. "My name is Officer Paxton. Is this your daughter?"

"Yes. This is my daughter, Josie," my dad responded.

The second officer looked at me and smiled. To my surprise, he said, "My niece has Down Syndrome. And she is way smarter than me." He paused then added, "And my name is Officer Ray."

I laughed and said, "My name is Josie, and sometimes I'm smarter than my dad." My dad's face blushed, as it often did whenever I said something unfiltered.

My mom extended her hand to Officer Ray. "Hi, my name is Alana, Josie's mother. And this is Oliver, Josie's dad." Officer Ray shook her hand and nodded his head, in my direction.

"Why don't you tell us what you saw?" Officer Ray transferred his hat under his right arm and pulled a small notebook from his jacket pocket. There was a pen attached to the notebook, which he grabbed and scribbled something onto a fresh page. He looked at me expectantly.

"I dreamt I was standing in the clouds. I saw a white van chasing a little girl. She was wearing a purple coat. The man in the van was wearing a dark brown hoodie sweater and hanging out of an open door. I saw the license plate was from Delaware, 6-3-0-Z-P-E. It looked like she was running in a zig-zag, and she hid in the neighbor's yard. That was all I saw."

"Wow. That's a lot of detail. Great memory!" said Officer Paxton, with enthusiasm.

Officer Ray chimed in, "Well, in addition to your call, we received a call from the little girl's parents. There was an attempted kidnapping, but she escaped." He continued, "She was too scared to remember more detail about the van or its occupants, so we thought we would speak with some of the neighbors."

My mom's stoic demeanor shuddered. Dad spoke first, "I'm really sorry. I feel like I should know who all of our neighbors are, but we just moved here from Alabama."

"This is usually a really safe area, with a low crime rate. We're all a little surprised and eager to help find these criminals. Despite Josie's details coming from a dream, I think we should start by running this license plate and see what we can come up with," Officer Paxton said.

"It wouldn't be the first time that Investigators have worked with a psychic or somebody who claims they see things in dreams," Officer Ray chimed in.

"Josie, is there anything else you can think of that might help point us in the right direction?" asked Officer Paxton.

"No, not at this time," I said.

"Okay, we're going to move on the information as soon as we leave here. In the meantime, keep a close eye on Josie and prevent another attempt. Call us if there is suspicious activity." Officer Paxton handed my dad a business card. "My cell phone number is on the back."

"Thank you so much, officers. We will keep an eye on Josie and introduce ourselves to the neighbors, so we can form a neighborhood watch."

"Sounds like a good idea. You folks have yourselves a nice day." Officer Ray and my dad shook hands, while my mom opened the door for them to exit. After they left, my dad walked up and hugged me.

"You heard what the officers said. Stay away from those abandoned lots, and make sure we know where you are at all times." My dad had a worried expression on his face.

"I'm pretty sure that's not what they said, but I understand, and I'll stay inside the next few days." I squeezed my dad's hand and then hugged my mom, who looked like she was on the verge of tears.

"Can you wait upstairs? Your father and I need to talk about how we'll introduce ourselves to the little girl's parents and what, if anything, we say about your dream."

Chapter 5

After the police visited, my parents met with the neighbors on our street and scheduled a four-week neighborhood watch. The family of the little girl in the purple coat went out of town, to stay safe with relatives. I was hoping to meet her and tell her my story.

My mom was supportive of my newfound gift of what she described as a spiritual awakening. She offered a visit with our Baptist Pastor, but then we agreed the church should not be involved yet. Especially, because we did not know if it was a one-time vision, a dream, or something else.

The next few days were uneventful, but Zeke and I stayed indoors as much as possible. My dad worked from home to keep a close eye on our family and our residence. We ordered a lot of pizza and doodled on the kitchen chalkboard. I heard my parents, downstairs, early in the morning, volunteering for the neighborhood watch. My dad's night watch was from nine to eleven p.m., and my mom's morning watch was from three to five a.m. Zeke protected me in the room, snuggled next to my pillow.

The officers returned with good news. They caught the man with the dark brown hooded sweater and the driver. A neighbor spotted them near a convenience store, where they were loading up with liquor. The perpetrators were brought downtown and interrogated. Although they confessed, there was still speculation about where they were from. Apparently, my mom heard they weren't carrying any form of identification. They were detained and later booked on numerous charges. Hopefully, the little girl and her family would feel safe enough to return home.

With news of the male perpetrators who were caught, the area seemed to liven up a little. People were outside barbecuing, washing cars, and playing street hockey. The weather cooperated, with less rain and thunderstorms. Pretty soon the lot across the street was visited by people carrying blueprints and wearing hard hats. As a thirteen-year-old, I suppose I would call them construction workers, but they seemed like they were business people.

I thought about joining them because I was stir-crazy, and I needed adventure. Instead, my mom offered another solution. Over dinner, she announced that we should go on a family vacation. The options were Disney World, two different cruise ships, or a four-day weekend in the St. Thomas Islands. The incident must have really scared my parents. Usually, we would not discuss vacation until June, and it was only March.

"My vote is a pet-friendly cruise," I casually said.

My dad responded, "I like the idea of a weekend in the St. Thomas Islands. We can rent a Bungalow and organize some water sports."

"Hmmm… I was going to say Disney World. I think a little escape from reality would do us all some good." My mom stood up from the kitchen table and made her way toward the cupboard. She grabbed three mugs and three saucers for hot cocoa. Unlike most people who purchase hot cocoa, we drank ours year-round. And my mom adds a little spice, from mixing cinnamon and nutmeg.

"I think Zeke should make the final decision. He can choose a vacation by barking." I swiveled in my seat and stared at Zeke. "Okay, Zeke. Bark once for Disney World, twice for a cruise and three times for St. Thomas Islands." I almost told them about Zeke having the ability to speak.

My dad put his hand up and said, "Wait. Why don't we just draw from a bowl? I'll write the vacation options on pieces of paper, crumple them up and then put them into a bowl." Zeke's tail was wagging because he thought we were talking about him. My dad stood up, to grab the paper and pen, and then he froze in mid-stride. At first, I thought he was joking, like a game of *Simon Says*.

But I quickly realized Zeke and I were the only ones moving. I looked around at my mom, and she was still holding the cocoa pouches. I felt my skin tingle, as a gentle breeze entered the room. I could not tell if I was afraid or just sensing a presence. Zeke did not seem scared.

I finally stood up and pushed at my dad's hand. His hand felt rigid and barely moved more than a ½ inch in either direction. What in the world was going on? The only thing I could think of was a time warp. Wait! Maybe the moon rock had something to do with this. I ran through the kitchen and leaped up the stairs. I saw that my room was glowing the familiar purple color, and the light was coming from the nightstand drawer. I pulled the jewelry box out and then opened the lid. The little spirals of silver light started to join the purple glow. I ran back downstairs holding the moon rock and entered the kitchen. There was a glint of sparkle in the air, surrounding the room. Suddenly, I heard our conversation from three minutes ago, but everything sounded like an echo.

I sat down in my chair and, instantly, the rubber band of time released, and my parents continued their conversation and movement. The effect was stronger than a feeling of déjà vu. While they continued to talk about vacation, I noticed something shining under the table. I sat back in my seat and glimpsed at the object that caught my attention. It was a silver shoe, with a delicate flower print. That was not there before! I bent down and picked it up, examining the shoe pattern.

"Go ahead and pick your vacation." My dad slid the bowl across the table. My mind was furthest from the task at hand, but I reached into the bowl. I grabbed a crumpled piece of paper and opened it. The scrap of paper said ST. THOMAS ISLANDS.

"St. Thomas Islands, yay!" I nervously yelped. My mom sat down with the cups of hot cocoa and handed me one.

"Here you go!" She smiled and pointed at the shoe. "What have you got there?"

"It was probably something Zeke found outside. I saw it under the table." I shrugged and looked at the shoe, as though it were a chew toy. Zeke was always bringing in toys from outside. But, usually, he would pile them into the corner of the room.

"Where is Zeke? I thought he was in here a minute ago." We both looked around the kitchen, but Zeke was elsewhere.

"He's probably still upstairs. He followed me up when I went to get the moon rock." As soon as I said it, I knew they would not understand. They were frozen in time, while Zeke and I were running around looking for a magic rock. Great. Hopefully, my mom didn't realize the absurdity of what I said.

"I have no idea what you're talking about. Finish your hot cocoa and then off to bed."

"I think I'll drink my hot cocoa upstairs and look for Zeke," I said, as I faked a yawn. "I'm really glad we're going to the St. Thomas Islands. Maybe I'll start packing." With that, I left the kitchen and went upstairs. Zeke was not in my room. After searching the remaining bedrooms and bathrooms, I realized he might be outside. I ran back down the stairs and opened the front door. It was dark outside, so I turned on the light.

"Zeke!" I paused but did not hear anything. There was a sinking feeling in my stomach as I thought about the time warp. I was afraid Zeke might be pulled into a different dimension without me. How would I explain that to my parents?

My dad joined me at the door and asked why I was looking outside. "He was just here a minute ago," he said. "Did you let him outside while I was putting the pieces of paper into the bowl?"

"Uh, yea," I said as calm as I could.

"Okay, but he should really walk with a leash." He went to the coat closet and grabbed a heavy-duty flashlight from the top shelf. He stepped outside into the chill weather and turned on the flashlight.

"I'm going with you," I said. I pulled my coat from the closet and ran outside, ahead of my dad. "Zeke!" I called out.

My dad was shining the flashlight around the driveway. "I'll look in the backyard. You stay here." He said. I waited a few minutes, until my dad returned. "That's strange. He wasn't in the backyard, and he's not responding to his name." We decided to walk further down the street, aiming the flashlight at all the shrubs, under cars, and in driveways. He was nowhere to be found, and my heart felt like it was skipping a few beats. I was worried.

My dad could sense the tension. "Don't worry, Josie. We'll find him." He patted me on the head and added, "Let's keep walking until the end of the street. If he doesn't show up then we'll jump in the car and search for him." He squeezed my arm, reassuringly.

We walked to the end of the street and, just as we were getting ready to turn around, we heard Zeke bark. He sounded as though he were quite a distance from us. My dad flicked the light in the general direction, ahead of us, near a large clearing between the trees.

"Okay. Stay close to me. He might be stuck in the field." I grabbed my dad's arm and followed his pace toward where the light was shining. Our neighborhood was not quite suburbia, but more of a suburban sprawl, as my mother described it. There were homes every few hundred yards. Plenty of space to play and easy for a dog to wander. Although, I still could not figure out how he escaped our home; I was sure I did not open the doors.

Upon closer look, Zeke was trotting out into the middle of a grassy area, barking at the sky. We made our way to him and followed his gaze. There, in the middle of the night sky, above our neighbor's home, a trail of light was blazing across the horizon. The light was pink and yellow, with a lot of steam around the edges of the object hurling its way toward land. My dad let out a gasp, and I involuntarily clung to his coat. Zeke was barking hysterically, enough that the neighbors turned on their porch light. Soon, the neighbors came out onto their porches, saw my dad's flashlight and called out into the night for a response.

"Hello, out there! Is everything alright?" said the home to our right.

My dad's voice cracked as he responded, "There's something in the air. It's flying toward us!"

The man and woman on the porch ran down the front steps and joined us, in what seemed like a few seconds. Their reactions summarized exactly what we should do. The elderly man put his arm around the woman and yelled, "Let's get out of its path!"

It was hard to tell where the object would land, but it looked like it would hit around where we were standing. My dad and I ran toward the line of trees, and Zeke followed. The older couple ran toward their house but stayed in front of the porch. All our eyes were focused on the incoming meteor, if that's what it was.

The meteor struck the ground and skid toward the line of trees opposite from where we were standing. The sound was enormous, and it seemed like sparks were flying everywhere the meteor made contact. All of us screamed, just as car alarms sounded and windows started imploding. The force of the impact knocked us onto our backs and sent Zeke dancing across the grass, like tumbleweed. He yelped a few times and then landed on his feet.

"Josie!" My dad sat up and clawed at the air. The flashlight was pointing at a tree.

"I'm right here!" I answered, and then I started sobbing. My whole body was shaking from the movement of air around the meteor. He made his way over to me and then gave me a gigantic hug. I could tell he was scared because his heart sounded like it was in his throat. Zeke ran up to us and stood on his hind legs, scratching at my dad's jeans. I picked him up and held him as we focused our attention on the meteor.

At this point, everyone in the neighborhood was streaming out of their houses to see what all the commotion was about. The elderly couple were sitting in the grass, but their expressions were unclear from our distance. "Are you gesture that said they were alive and probably stunned from seeing a meteor streak through the sky.

With caution, I walked up to the meteor while my dad was retrieving the flashlight. He turned around, saw me and yelled in protest, "Stay back! That could be dangerous." But Zeke and I were already examining the texture of the rock. It was glowing red and looked like the exact same structure as the moon rock I found – with a smooth surface and sponge content.

My dad made his way up to us and shone the flashlight along the path of the meteor. The entire field was bathed in fog and some kind of electrical current. People started entering the field to inspect what landed. That was when my dad decided to back up and grab ahold of me. We headed to the street, with Zeke in tow. Neither of us spoke on the walk home. My mom apparently heard the deafening roar and was already walking in our direction. She was carrying her own flashlight and calling out our names. We met in the middle of the street and hugged. "Mom, we just saw a meteor land near the Jones' house."

Without missing a beat, my mom said, "I told them those cable satellites were too powerful." I laughed nervously, despite myself. In the distance, we could hear sirens as we made our way back to the driveway.

Chapter 6

It was hours after the police and fire trucks showed up that we finally went to bed. We were exhausted from all the excitement. Nothing that dramatic had ever happened to us before and the neighbors spoke about everything from alien invasions to foreign nuclear meteors. At one point, I wondered if we would ever be able to visit St. Thomas Islands, at the rate these strange occurrences were taking place.

As I relaxed in bed, my mind wandered to the similarities between the moon rock and the meteor. It seemed only logical that the meteor split into shards and pieces of it probably landed around our neighborhood a few days prior. But, what kind of meteor opens other dimensions? From everything that I studied about space, a lot of the incoming meteor particles are little fragments from a lively universe. How would we know what each meteor is capable of?

If I could talk to Stephen Hawking, I would tell him that I think about the Universe as a Bach composition. Math might not be the coolest subject, but music makes sense. Each of the planets, in our galaxy, is a representation of a lyre. Some dark and cool, while others are bright and warm. That is how I would explain our solar system to a blind person or to somebody who thinks the Universe is just a boring paint canvas. Seeing a meteor up close was like having a front-row seat to the fabric of space and time. And with that thought, I drifted into sleep.

I was in the middle of a forest, where the grass was tall and the color of wheat. The grass was swaying side to side, in a gentle pulsating rhythm. The night sky was a combination of magenta, periwinkle, and peach. In the distance, I heard a songbird making its way to where I was standing. There was a strand of pearls flowing from its mouth and dancing above the blades of grass. Each pearl contained a little droplet of gold liquid, like honey. The bird suspended itself in mid-air, directly in front of me, and at eyesight. I am pretty sure it was a hummingbird, though I had only seen one in a television documentary. The hummingbird was trying to tell me something because the beak kept pointing upward, in a flicking motion. I looked up and saw a ripple in the air, that seemed to be magnifying into a large circle of light. I squinted my eyes and tried to find the lines outlining the object that was flying toward us.

There it was – the same meteor from earlier this evening, but a different color. This one was a bright orange ball of magnificence. It was radiating shades of orange I had not seen before. The edges of the space rock were a little blurred, almost as though the rock had invisible wings that were causing the surrounding ripples.

It landed in the field, in front of me. The hummingbird hovered above the rock and then lowered itself. The meteor responded and its flat mid-surface became a dense liquid. The bird flew into the center of the meteor, its wings causing ripples. I felt the ground vibrate under my feet, as though the earth were responding to this supernatural opening. Whoa! It actually felt like the earth was communicating with the bird and meteor.

I stepped forward and admired the rock's beauty, which reminded me of a colorful diffuser. As I was examining the exterior, the meteor projected an image into the air around me. It was like a 3D vision of our neighborhood. Each house was represented with a color, or combination of colors. One home was glowing purple. I recognized the building as the area where the little girl was almost abducted. I remembered how in my dream vision there was no purple color. It was the only color missing from the rainbow path. But now, there it was, highlighting somebody's house and yard. The vision focused on the bedroom window, where the girl was sleeping. This was the first time I saw a detailed version of her. She looked like she might be Mediterranean, with long curly hair, and light brown skin. She was curled up with a pillow and sleeping peacefully.

She rustled in her bed and then slowly opened her eyes. She was looking in my direction, but I wasn't sure if she saw me. She groggily stood up, put her shoes on, and walked toward the bedroom window. Her hand extended past the wall and into the outside night air because the wall was no longer solid. She was smiling, as though she were familiar with this routine. Next, her leg extended outside of the window, and then she pushed herself to exit her home. This whole scene was very reminiscent of my experience with the glowing moon rock and rainbow path.

Speaking of the rainbow path, there it was – a pastel road connecting our homes. She walked the length of the path and then entered the side of my house. I knew it was my house because I recognized the willow tree. The vision, if that's what this was, zoomed and magnified the girl's actions. She was entering our kitchen, at the exact moment that my parents and I were talking about vacation. My mom was reaching for the packets of cocoa just as she slid under the kitchen table and listened to our banter. She reached up and scratched something onto the underside of the table with a coin.

My dad was walking back to where I had been sitting, holding the pieces of paper where we wrote our vacation ideas. The girl saw him and probably thought he would shift the chairs and sit. She turned around and tried to squeeze between the chairs. In the process, she lost her shoe. She did not seem to notice because she crawled from her position and stood up. She didn't glance backward as she exited the room and rejoined the rainbow path. She skipped home, walked into her room, kicked her shoe off, and crawled into bed.

The projection ended, and the hummingbird floated out of the center of the meteor. For a moment, I wondered if the meteor was a door to another world. The bird started singing, and the song sounded like the 'o' vowel sound, at different vibration levels. Then the bird stopped singing and spoke, "Find the girl with the shoe and purple coat. She knows about other worlds and is a guardian of a portal above your home. There is danger from another planet. The two of you must meet and find the second talisman. I will return with further instructions." At that, she fluttered into the unbelievably gorgeous air, mixed with a kaleidoscope of colors. I noticed the meteor was vibrating, and its center was no longer fluid, but changing back to its natural state. I could see there was a small chunk missing from the side of the meteor. I leaned in closer and saw the outline was the approximate size and shape of the rock sitting in my nightstand table. Well, now I know where the rock came from. I wondered if it was glowing back in my room.

Chapter 7

The next morning, I woke up to the smell of fresh bacon cooking downstairs. I could just picture my mom dancing around the stove and Zeke scouring the floor for scraps. Zeke had a knack for weaving between my mom's feet, while she was in motion. Sometimes, she would accidentally kick him or step on his paw. It was weird how he never learned his lesson.

I anxiously jumped out of bed and made my way downstairs. It looked like dad was working from his home office, across from the living room. He was an urban landscape architect. He was sitting at his desk and eyeballing some of his open sketch pads. Some of the sketches were framed along the walls, between the rows of bookcases filled with books and miniature size buildings. He once told me that he dreamt of geometric shapes and patterns, instead of sheep.

"Mornin' sunshine. I started work early so that Mom could have the kitchen to herself. She was listening to her iPod tunes and speaking way too loud," he said.

"Is she still listening to that indie pop music?" I asked, referring to my mom's recent fascination with lesser-known artists and the Independent Film Channel.

"Yup," he responded, with emphasis on the 'p' sound.

"Go in there and grab yourself a plate. I'll join you guys in a few minutes."

I exited his office and walked into the kitchen just as my mom was setting plates of food in the center of the table. I loved this time of day when the sunlight highlighted the white cabinets and reflected from all the glass. This was my favorite part of our house: the large kitchen with a medium-sized breakfast nook. I grabbed a round plate from one of the cabinets and started piling on the food: fluffy eggs, bacon, French toast, and strawberries.

Still humming her favorite tunes, my mom walked up to me and planted a big kiss on the top of my head. "Good morning, buttercup." She had been calling me that for as long as I could remember. The story goes that when I was five, she put me in a yellow dress, and we spent the day filling a basket with only buttercup flowers. They were the smallest and hardest to find amongst all the grass, shrubs, and other wildflowers. Once our basket was full, we plucked the tops of the flowers and smeared them under our chins, making up silly words that rhymed with butter or cup.

"Mom," I said. "I'd like to go to the library today and research meteors." Although that was only three-quarters of the truth, I did intend to go to the library. But my current plan was to find the little girl with the purple coat and invite her to come along.

"That's fine with me, but I'm driving," she said sternly.

She sat down to eat and then ruffled my hair. "There's been a whole lot of commotion around here. Maybe we should think about our vacation and the timing of when we would like to go." With that, she put a forkful of bacon and eggs into her mouth.

"I'll think about it." I pushed the food around on my plate while thinking of ways that I could avoid being driven to the library. Maybe my mom would be agreeable to stopping in at the little girl's house. Although, she would probably wonder how I knew where she lived.

"Mom, would it be okay if I just walk to the library? It's a nice day outside, and I like thinking and walking. Besides, they caught the guys who did it." I looked at her with anticipation.

My mom stayed silent and set her fork down. She looked at me with motherly concern and then smiled.

"Josie, you've been independent since the age of three. I respect that about you. And I hope you respect my concern and care for you. Yes, they caught the guys who did it. But that doesn't mean the impact of what they tried to do hasn't affected this entire neighborhood."

She paused. "I'll let you walk to the library, as long as you call me along the way and call me when you arrive. Then, I am going to time you… Let's say two hours of library time, and you call me as you're heading home. Can you remember all that?"

"Yes. I might stop at the little girl's house and introduce myself to her parents," I said truthfully.

"Well, if that's your plan then I should go with you. Both dad and I should go with you, so we can all introduce ourselves."

"Can we do that tonight? I'll just go to the library this afternoon," I said.

"Let me speak with your father and see if he can set aside some time. I'm also going to find their phone number and make sure it's all right for us to just pop in."

I finished eating my plate of food and stood up to put my dish in the sink. I saw my mom's reflection in the window, above the sink. She was watching me with the look only a mother can give – the focused stare of a protective lioness.

The walk to the library was refreshingly quiet. On the way there, I saw that the field where the meteor landed was sectioned off with yellow tape. There were men and women wearing face masks, gloves, and long rubber boots. Some of the people were taking samples from the meteor, whilst others were measuring the trail of impact. In daylight, the scene looked like a small plane crash. There were still a few stragglers, from the neighborhood, walking around and taking pictures. The meteor excitement was featured in the national news.

I figured at the library I would be able to find out more about our town's history and if this was the first time a meteor had ever landed in our area. I could just google the information, but I really wanted to explore the library. I loved the smell of paper, wood, and old books. There was also something about the way each person was absorbed in their own story. All of these people were sitting near each other and yet they were worlds apart, exploring mathematics, other planetary systems, or learning a new language.

At the library, I went straight to the history section. There was a kiosk with a computer, where I could research the topic and then find the location of the books. According to the keyword search, the book I was looking for was titled, *Carrington's Supernatural History*. That was odd. How would a meteor be considered supernatural? After looking at the rows of books, I found the range of Dewey decimals that matched the computer results. The book was sitting on the top shelf, which was outside of my reach. I found a step stool and slid it over to the section I was interested in and climbed up. The area I was looking at was undisturbed, as though nobody had touched the row since the library's grand opening, eighty years before our family moved here. The smell of aged paper was much more pronounced, as I stood up and grabbed the book's spine. It slid out with hesitation, the laminate sticking to the sides of the surrounding books.

I lowered myself and put the step stool back. There was a small area in the corner of the library, where I could sit and read. The first page I looked for was the Table of Contents. The Preface is where I wanted to start because it would give me some background information.

I skimmed the pages and stopped when I read the following paragraph:

According to local legend, the town is centered below a spacial vortex. There have been several reports of people entering Langdon field and exiting on the other side of town. Their memories were either erased, or the teletransportation happened so quickly that their minds could not comprehend. On several occasions, a stray animal would appear out of nowhere, scaring nearby picnickers. One of the strays was an animal that was reported missing three months earlier. Residents were certain that the area around Langdon field was haunted.

Interesting. I read the paragraph again, to make sure I did not miss anything. Sometimes, my extra chromosome made reading difficult, but I always pushed past the challenges. Now, I would have to try and find the connection between meteors and Langdon field, or meteors, and vortexes. I went to the computer, typed in 'vortex' and only two results appeared. One of the books was available online, and all I had to do was click a link. The page loaded and the Table of Contents appeared. I laughed aloud as I saw one of the first chapter headings was, 'What is a Vortex?' The paraphrased explanation of a vortex was as follows:

An area of supernatural activity, unexplained disappearances and reappearances, time distortion, and spacial magnification. Scientists have explained vortexes as a disruption in the earth's magnetic field.

Hmmm. Maybe that would explain why the meteor landed near our home. The vortex could be a kind of space magnet, pulling in objects from beyond our earth's atmosphere. I had seen that in a space documentary. Therefore, the meteor would technically be extraterrestrial.

I printed the page with the vortex definition and scanned the book's barcode, along with my library card. As I was leaving, I noticed a tall, slender boy wearing a baseball cap. He was standing behind a row of books and peering at me with curiosity. I would not have paid him attention, except his baseball cap spelled a word and color I was recently quite captivated with: PURPLE.

I was just about to walk near him when he pivoted and went in the opposite direction. Well, maybe he was not that curious. I redirected myself to the library exit and made my way outside, into the brilliant sunshine.

After about five minutes, I was rounding the corner and staring up at the little girl's house. It was a brick front, with vinyl sides and large white shutters. The door was painted a dark blue, with a brass doorknob. I reached for the doorbell and realized it was one of those fancy, digital contraptions. They probably installed it after the van incident.

The doorbell sounded like a musical composition and then the screen above the doorbell illuminated. "Who is it?" I heard from the intercom.

"My name is Josie. I live down the street." I waved at the camera.

"Oh, hey Josie! We just spoke to your mom. Hang tight, and I'll be right there." The mother, if that's who I was speaking to, sounded friendly. A few seconds later, the door opened, and I was greeted by a bright-eyed woman. She extended her hand and said, "I'm Isabel, Cilantra's mom."

I shook her hand and responded, "You're beautiful. I've never met Cilantra – that's why I'm here. That's a cool name." Isabel smiled and motioned for me to come in.

"My mom doesn't know I'm here because she and my dad wanted to come tonight," I confided.

"Yes, she mentioned you would be visiting together. Why don't we do a quick introduction and then you can be on your way. Cilantra is upstairs, playing teatime with her dolls. Why don't you come in and wait in the kitchen?" I followed her into the well-lit kitchen, which was crowded with plants, flowers, and pottery. The smells reminded me of a botanical garden. Isabel walked to the refrigerator and pulled out a plate of cookies.

"Let me throw these into the microwave and pour you a glass of milk. How does that sound?"

"Delicious," I said.

I watched as she danced around the kitchen with ease and elegance. Within a matter of minutes, she placed the cookies and a glass of milk in front of me. "I'll be right back. Let me tell Cilantra you're here, and she'll join you at the table." I nodded my approval and reached for a cookie.

The cookies tasted like marshmallows and peanut butter. The combination made me drool a little. And the nice cold milk was just what I needed to balance the flavors. Sometimes milk was a better hydrator than water. Especially, on a day like today – not too cold and not too hot. I was looking at the condensation on the glass when from upstairs I heard Cilantra's voice, "I know who Josie is." I paused mid-bite and knew this would be an interesting conversation.

Chapter 8

Cilantra and her mom entered the downstairs kitchen area, where we spent five minutes speaking about uninteresting topics because Isabel was in the room. In person, she seemed older than how she appeared in the dreams. She was probably only eight or nine years old.

My phone beeped with a text alert. My mom was checking in to make sure I was safe.

"Well, I only wanted to stop in and introduce myself because I dreamed about you. My parents are planning a visit soon," I said and then realized I mentioned the dream.

"You dreamed of me?" Cilantra asked.

"Uh, yea. It was a quick dream," I said.

"I remember the officer saying something about a teenager who dreamt of the perps' license plates. Was that you?" Cilantra's mom seemed relieved.

"Yes, ma'am." I shuffled my feet and looked uncomfortably at the floor.

"In this household, we believe in dreams and intuition. That's probably what saved Cilantra's life."

"I'm glad you're safe." I looked at Cilantra, who was smiling and scoping out my satchel of books. "I should really be going. My mom texted, and she sounds worried."

"Okay, I'll walk you outside," Cilantra said as we maneuvered toward the front of the house. Her mom patted my shoulder and said, "It was nice to meet you. Visit soon," then walked down the long hall to the kitchen.

As soon as Cilantra and I were alone, she squeezed my hand. "I have something to show you." I smiled and felt a warm flutter in my heart, feeling as though Cilantra and I would be instant friends. Instead of going outside, she led me to the sunroom, where there was a wicker loveseat and matching wicker chairs. The sunroom was floor to ceiling glass, with a desk nestled in the corner and a tall desk lamp. There was a beanbag chair next to the metal coffee table. Cilantra plopped down into the bag of proverbial beans and reached behind the loveseat to pull out another one. I plopped down into mine and accidentally belched.

Cilantra laughed and then forced herself to burp as well.

I shrugged my shoulders and laughed. "The surgeries from my Down Syndrome make me fart and burp a lot."

"My mom's cooking makes me fart and burp a lot," Cilantra said. We both laughed. "What kind of surgeries?" She looked at me with concern.

I pulled up my shirt and showed her the scars, while explaining, "The long scar is from open-heart surgery, to repair tiny holes. The diagonal one is from repairing my intestines."

"Oh, wow! That must have hurt. You're healed now?" She leaned her head to the side, with a furrowed brow.

"Yea, I'm fine. Totally healed." I lowered my shirt and changed the subject. "Your house is really pretty."

"Thanks! I like our house. It's a place that makes me feel warm and safe." She paused and then added, "I have something I wanted to show you." She reached under the couch and grabbed a piece of white construction paper. She handed it to me and said, "Does this look familiar?"

I looked at the piece of paper and saw a drawing of a meteor, surrounded with swirls of color. "Hey! That's from my dream." Cilantra nodded her head with understanding. "That's the night I dreamt that you went into our home and were listening to our conversation, in the kitchen." She smiled and had the appearance of someone wise beyond her years. I continued, "And I dreamt of the van who was chasing you the night after it happened. I saw you outrun the guys and hide in the neighbor's yard. You were wearing a purple coat."

"Yea, I was afraid they would catch me, and then I remembered that Mrs. Walsh's fence has two panels missing next to the gate. I squeezed in just in time." She shuddered at the remembrance of the close call. Then she sat up straight and with a serious expression said, "While I was hiding in the neighbors' yard, I looked up at the sky and saw a glimmering silhouette, just above one of the power lines. After I went home and told my parents and the police, I snuggled in bed with my parents. I only dreamt about a minute, but it was of you and your dog. It looked like you chased away the bad men."

"That would be my dog, Zeke. He was there with me when the arm appeared from the air, and a rainbow path opened in my room. He spoke to me, and I understood him. Anyway, we saw the men in the van, and I started shouting at them. I wasn't sure if anybody heard me," I pressed on. "And I know this sounds weird, but earlier that day, I found a piece of meteor across the street from our home. It was glowing and that was when the rainbows first appeared. I was staring at everything like I was in a dream. At some point, I heard a voice say, 'HELP HER!'"

"Wait. So, you have been having rainbow visions, too?" she asked.

"Only since finding the moon rock, or meteor – whatever it is."

"You've been protecting me, and I didn't even know it. You're like my hero." She leaned in and squeezed me with a hug.

I said, "But the rock and my dog, Zeke, might be the true heroes. Zeke found the rock and the meteor."

"The meteor appeared to me in a dream and spoke. It said there was a portal above our town. I'm not sure what a portal is, but it sounds dangerous," she said.

"I just came back from the library and printed a definition of a portal, or what they call a vortex. The portal is interfering with the earth's magnetic field and pulling space objects from the atmosphere." I reached into the satchel and showed her one of the books.

"Really? That sounds like a sci-fi movie," she said.

"In my dream about the meteor, I saw a singing and talking hummingbird. She flew inside of the meteor and activated a projection system. The air around me was filled with images of you walking into our home and the same rainbow path I saw from my first vision." I stood up from the beanbag chair and started pacing around the room, with excitement. I continued my story, forgetting about my mom's previous text. "The hummingbird said there was a portal above our town and that bad people, from another planet, were trying to access it. She said you and I were supposed to meet and find a third tall man, or something like that."

"A third tall man? Sounds weird, but okay." She shrugged her shoulders.

Suddenly, we heard a commotion outside, and there was a fluttering of doorbell rings. We got up from our seats and ran toward the front of the house. Isabel gave us a stern look and told us to wait in the living room. She approached the door and said, "Yes, who is it?"

"I'm the USPS delivery man, and I have an unusual package here."

"Could you please step away from the front porch so I can see your truck?" Isabel stood firm against the door and stared at the doorbell's inside display screen as the USPS guy stepped back a few spaces. After she saw the truck, she said, "Okay, good. Hold on a moment." She opened the door, and the USPS person started rambling.

"It's the strangest thing. I was putting this small package into the mailbox, and it started jumping in my hand. I dropped it, and the package started glowing and making a weird chirping sound." He held the bubble wrap envelope up for us to see.

It was addressed to Cilantra, but her mom took it from his hand and inspected the writing.

"I'll open it," she said and ran her finger along the inside of the corner and length of the crease. She turned the package upside down, and a zipper fell out.

It was the length of a finger and about half an inch thick. It was a light copper color with blue trim. The zipper was silent. When it did not shimmer, the mailman huffed a little and said, "Well, please tell the person or company who sent the zipper to package it the right way. If there are batteries included, then they should be in separate wrapping.”

“I see,” said Isabel. “Where is the sender address?”

“That’s strange. We don’t deliver packages unless there’s a sender address. Would you mind if I take a picture of it, and I’ll check with my Inventory Manager?”

“Sure. We’ll hold on to the zipper, and you take the package. Let us know what you find out.” Isabel handed him the small envelope and put the large zipper in her pocket. She smiled, thanked the man for alerting her, and then closed the door.

“Mom, why would somebody send me a zipper?” Cilantra held out her hand.

“I don’t know. Could this be from one of your friends at dad’s golf club?”

“No. Not at all. We don’t send each other things like that.” Cilantra frowned, and I took my cue that it was time to leave.

Chapter 9

Before heading home, I asked Cilantra for her phone number and then texted her my number. Then, I texted my mom and told her I was on the way to our home. I walked as quickly as possible, wondering if I should tell my parents about my visit. I also thought about how since finding the moon rock, weird things kept happening around me, and apparently, around Cilantra.

I walked through the front door and realized no one was home, except for myself and Zeke. He greeted me at the front door, with a lot of tail wagging. Just then, I remembered what I wanted to do. I entered the kitchen and crawled under the table. After looking up, I saw the words 'St. Thomas Islands' scratched into the underside of the wood.

The house felt empty so I decided I would make a snack. There was a note on the refrigerator from my mom saying that she was at the grocery store and would be home soon. She decorated the note with stickers and smiley faces – much better than texting emoticons. The note also said tonight was taco night, so she was purchasing fresh ingredients.

All I could think about was a banana split. I pulled the chocolate, strawberry, and vanilla ice cream from the freezer and then found the chocolate syrup in the refrigerator. Zeke knew I was up to something and sat at my feet. I almost dropped the bowl and resisted the urge to step on his toes. I grabbed a spoon from the drawer and went to work on my masterpiece.

Five minutes later, the banana split was devoured. I saved a little slice for Zeke, who was salivating. First, I licked all the chocolate syrup off from around the edges and then I placed the banana on the floor. Zeke snapped it up with his tongue and swallowed it whole.

"Zeke, I think we should lounge today. Mom put all my assignments in the study, but I would rather concentrate on my rock situation and read more of this book." I put the satchel in front of me and slowly removed the first book about supernatural happenings in Carrington.

I studied the book until Mom came home, yelling to help her unload the car. It was a welcome diversion. Some of the book's vocabulary was a little too steep for me. My general sense was that nobody could explain why or how our town was supernatural. There were lots of theories about sun flares and meteors, but nothing concrete, about the vortex.

I helped my mom put the groceries away and then excused myself to start on my lesson plan. My study area was like another sanctuary, with cool blue walls and beach pictures. I remember picking out the floor rug, as though it were an article of clothing. It was a pretty peach color with a paisley blue, maroon, and tan print. I liked it because it matched some of the colors from the picture.

Today, I was learning about punctuation and decimals. I did not mind school. However, with all of the excitement from the meteor and meeting Cilantra, I was determined to make sense of the mystery. I was passing most of my classes with A and B grades. Yet, here I was, struggling to make sense of what I was reading. I was repeatedly reading the same phrases so I could absorb the lessons and pass the quizzes.

After what seemed like hours, I finally released myself from the study, with my completed lessons in a neat pile. My mom would usually grade them before bedtime and then we would meet in the morning to cover incorrect answers. On Thursdays, I joined a study group, which doubled as a book club. That was where I could interact with other Down Syndrome teens, away from the usual teenage angst.

Dinner was ready, and I could smell the seasoned ground beef from upstairs. I ran to the kitchen just as dad entered from the garage. He gave me a quick hug and hung his car keys under the chalkboard.

"Sorry, I'm late," he said. "I had to drop off the designs at our client's house."

Mom gave him a big smooch on the lips, and I saw him tap her butt. They were always grabbing at each other, as though I weren't in the room. It was cute, I guess, in a grown-up kind of way.

I helped Mom set the table and made sure Zeke had food and water in his bowl. That would usually prevent him from jumping into the chairs. We sat down to eat and stuffed brown taco meat into flour tortilla rolls. There were bowls of guacamole, salsa, cheese, sour cream, and tomatoes. I love Taco Tuesdays! It was a nice break from the usual peanut butter and jelly sandwiches or pasta. My mom was an okay cook with some stuff and a really good cook with the traditional Brazilian dishes, or my dad's favorite meals.

"How was your day?" My dad asked after slurping freshly squeezed lemonade.

"Good. I went to the library and researched information about meteors. Then I went to the Schroeder's house and introduced myself to Cilantra for the first time." I paused, knowing they would inquire about my visit.

Sure enough, "I thought we agreed we would go as a family," my mom said.

"I'm sorry. I wasn't going to, but then her home was along the way. I thought I would offer my friendship since Cilantra barely escaped those creeps."

"Not only did you not respond to my text, but you went ahead and met with her family." I could hear the displeasure in her voice, and my dad chimed in to support her sentiment.

"Josie, we've spoken about this before. You need to stay in communication with us whenever you're outside of this home. That was part of the agreement for your cell phone. Remember?" my dad said in a stern voice.

"I said I was sorry. It won't happen again." I focused on my taco.

"Well, I called them this afternoon, while you were hopefully at the library." She raised her eyebrow at me then continued. "They've invited us to their home on Thursday, after Josie's study group. I accepted their invitation and offered to bring dessert."

"That was sweet of you," my dad said with a tinge of sour cream on his mustache.

I laughed and pointed at his face. "There's a smidge of sour cream on your 'stache," I said, trying to navigate the conversation in a more lighthearted direction.

Chapter 10

Cilantra and I spoke about our plans to meet up on Thursday. While our parents were socializing, we would compare notes, look at the rock, and try to visit the meteor. I was excited about having the opportunity to speak with her more about my meteor vision. I hadn't told my parents because they were already on edge about my kidnapping dream.

In preparation for our Thursday meeting, I started sketching and writing about the dream visions and the meteor encounter from Langdon field. A few of the pages were dedicated to research summaries. I cut out and pasted the definition of the vortex and included contact information for supernatural investigators underneath. The fact that I found supernatural investigators was really funny. I was not sure if I would ever call them, but it was nice to know that somebody had the equipment to measure weirdness.

I put the journal and jewelry box inside my backpack. Since we were going to be meeting at her house, I wanted to make sure I wouldn't forget any of the items. Maybe I could put Zeke inside, too. Cilantra would love him. Maybe my parents would let me bring him to Cilantra's house, or I could just invite her here, for a sleepover.

Now that the preparation was out of the way, I could focus on my studies. I read as much as possible and completed two days' worth of assignments. It was important for me to stay ahead of the academic curve because I had a feeling that the meteor excitement was just starting. Knowing me, I would obsess about researching both natural and supernatural phenomena. It was not my fault that I liked science fiction. My dad was a bit of a Star Trek nerd. He watched Star Trek reruns like a kid watches Power Rangers – in total awe.

After my studies, I looked around the room and tried to find something to do. I noticed my stack of oranges and a box of craft materials. Apples were easy to decorate because of their smooth surface. On the other hand, gluing anything to the skin of an orange was challenging because the pores were coarse. I looked at my collection of animated oranges, each resembling a certain type of personality: surfer, farmer, hairdresser, preacher. Maybe what my orange family needs is a dog. I decided I would make the ears out of cotton balls and the tail from wire piping. I would give him a black eye and name him 'Pea Brain'.

I opened the plain wooden box, decorated with glitter and magic markers. I opened it and saw I was low on gorilla glue. Only the gorilla glue could hold the objects in place on the orange's skin. Next to the bottle of glue, there was a pile of cotton balls, plastic eyes of all shapes, sizes and colors, and various materials.

Ever since I was a little girl, I loved different textures. I would walk around the doctor's office scratching my nails along the wallpaper or seat cushions. Then I started interacting with nature. I would run my fingers along tree bark, tickle my cuticles with blades of grass, and wiggle my toes in water. My mom said I was more inquisitive than most toddlers, demanding lots of sensory input.

I went downstairs and found the crate of oranges in our food pantry. I plucked two of them and returned upstairs, with a design in mind. First, I found red construction paper. Then, I drew a cape with the letter Z. His name would be 'Super Z', instead of 'Pea Brain'. Next, I drew his facial features, with big brown eyes and a cute little button nose. I cut the shape of my dog's cape and made two rectangular incisions, where the string would hold up each side. The finished product was a cute version of my dog, Zeke.

I was just about to take a picture when the small piece of meteor started glowing in my backpack. I removed the jewelry box and opened it. The rock was a silver color this time, and it was vibrating. I grabbed ahold of it and waited. No visions appeared, and the walls did not open with a rainbow path. Instead, the floor transitioned from wood to a translucent liquid. I was standing above my parents and watching them maneuver from the kitchen into the living room. It looked like they were getting ready to watch a movie. Within a matter of seconds, the floor changed back to the wood color and texture.

Now, I was anxious to go to sleep and step into another dream vision.

Chapter 11

After that uneventful night, three months passed and not one vision or shimmering rock. Every morning, I remained in bed, staring at the ceiling, waiting for the rainbow colors to open into the heavens. And every night, I rubbed the magical rock, hoping it would glow and reveal ancient secrets. I started to wonder if maybe everything temporarily shut down because I spoke about it to Cilantra. Or did the magic only happen when there was trouble around?

Despite the quiet rock, within that amount of time, Cilantra and I became best friends. We went everywhere together: the library, grocery stores, pet boutiques, and thrift stores. We found lots of books with supernatural and magical themes. We were looking for specific cases where somebody reported a portal or vortex encounter. We found two, but they were from 50+ years ago. And in both instances, they were adults with excellent reputations.

The excerpt read:

November 3, 1940. Kelsey Schmitz was driving home from work, on the East side of Langdon field. She saw an atmospheric disturbance, in the North-East corridor, where it appeared like localized lightning was hitting the same patch of

Earth. She swerved, thinking the lightning was heading in her direction and crashed her car into a parked vehicle. First responders arrived on the scene, where Kelsey was hysterical and pointing at the field. After they assessed she was not injured, they began writing notes of what Kelsey witnessed. At that point, the lightning had already stopped. But when the police investigated the area, they found burnt markings and the air smelled of dense ozone.

October 16, 1952. Maxime Croix was walking home from work and cut across Langdon field, in the lower South West corridor. She heard a songbird, but it was too dark to determine where it was coming from. The familiar bird twitter morphed into words of a song. There was no one else in the field, so she presumed it was music coming from a neighbor's house. Suddenly, a bright light appeared in front of her and knocked her to her knees. She reached into her purse and pulled out her work tape recorder, from being a Legal Aid. She pressed record and caught five seconds of unintelligible speech. She reported the field disturbance to the police and let them listen to the supernatural gibberish. The police searched the field with flashlights and found something in the reported area. There was a yellow stone with a unicorn engraving. When the first officer picked it up, it was hot to the touch. He yelped and dropped it, momentarily, in the grass. The officer said it was probably a teenager playing pranks and gave Maxime the rock.

Since reading those entries, our excitement grew because we realized we weren't the only ones who saw and heard supernatural things in Langdon field, or who had experienced atmospheric disturbance. Cilantra and I immediately began searching for the two witnesses. We were not sure if the individuals still lived in Carrington, but we decided we would start with the Yellow Pages and eventually work our way to an online search.

Cilantra was also trying to find the sender of the unusual zipper. So far, the only comparable gadgets seemed to be from faraway places, like Japan. I couldn't imagine someone from Japan randomly sending a nine-year-old a vibrating, chirping zipper. It had to be somebody who was familiar with our circumstances. Glowing rocks, dancing zippers, rainbow paths into a different dimension… that kind of thing.

Just then, my phone rang. It was Cilantra because I recognized the ring tone as, "This is my fight song…" I answered on the first ring and could hear Cilantra's heavy breathing. She sounded excited.

"Josie! I found one of them!" she exclaimed.

"One of who?" I asked.

"Maxime, from the book. I found her!" She laughed and then dropped the phone.

"Hello? Where is she?" I inquired, as Cilantra fumbled with the phone.

"Hey, did you hear what I said?" she repeated.

"Yes, where is she?" I was starting to feel frustrated at repeating myself.

"She's near the edge of town, a few blocks away from the old boathouse. I looked up her address online, from her first name. She was married and kept her married name. Maxime Dupont. According to the online report, she is eighty-eight years old."

"Wow! That's like, ancient." I said, "What if she doesn't remember the experience from Langdon field?"

"Well, there's only one way to find out. Can you meet me at my house in twenty minutes?"

"I think so. I'll call you right back." With that, I hung up the phone and ran downstairs. Mom was making dinner, and it was only twelve fifteen. It was a complicated meal, with mashed cauliflower. Sometimes Mom's health diets were a little intense, but usually, it was a yummy result.

"Mom, can I go to Cilantra's house for the afternoon? My assignments are complete, and I took out the trash this morning." I could hear the pleading in my own voice.

"That's fine. Take your phone with you. And be back at four so you can walk Zeke and wash up for suppertime."

"Okay. I will." I started to exit the kitchen.

"Wait a minute," Mom said. "Let me see your phone."

I walked back into the kitchen and handed her my phone, with an inquisitive look on my face.

"Your phone is at 12% battery power. Either power up the phone before leaving or take the charger with you."

"Yes, ma'am." I blushed and felt a sudden rush of love for my mom and her overprotectiveness. I lunged at her with open arms and gave her a hug. "I love you, Mom."

She squeezed me and said, "I love you, too."

With that, I went upstairs and called Cilantra.

"I'm on my way. Remind me to charge my phone."

Chapter 12

Before leaving our home, I grabbed the now dormant rock and put it in my pocket. My heart felt like it was skipping a few beats, as I jogged to Cilantra's home. She was pacing back and forth on the front porch, with a huge smile on her face and a backpack slung over her shoulder.

"I called Maxime and spoke with her adult son. He said she speaks like a wise old lady and remembers everything. He's heard the story about the yellow rock and said she'll be excited to talk to us about it." She grabbed my hand and off we went.

We walked fast and spoke little.

"My mom said I can only stay out for two hours. I had to give her the address of where we're going. She offered to drive, but I said it would be more fun if we walked," Cilantra said.

"I agree."

It was a ten-minute walk to Maxime's house, near the last street in Carrington's district. Ahead of us was a big grey boathouse that was restored and kept preserved as part of Carrington's history. To the right, there was a communal garden, with stone steps that led to the river. Maxime's house was in a cul-de-sac, around the corner from the garden.

The home looked very warm and inviting. It was one of those houses that looks like it is one level on the front side and is two levels on the back side, with a sloping hill. I could see from our distance that the backyard led to a pier, where there were two chairs seated near a hammock. Cilantra walked up to the front door first and rang the doorbell.

A short, bald man with a beard answered the door.

"You must be Cilantra. My mother's been waiting for you in the living room. My name is Stewart or Stew for short."

"Hey Stew, this is my best friend, Josie." She gestured toward me, and I waved awkwardly.

He opened the door and exposed a well-lit hallway, with tons of pictures aligning the walls. We stepped inside and were greeted with the scent of fresh laundry.

"What kind of detergent do you use?" I asked, wanting to make myself comfortable before meeting his elderly mother.

Stew laughed. "Um, I'm pretty sure we use Tide with some kind of 99 cent fabric softener."

"It smells good in here, like clean laundry and dryer sheets." Stew looked at me the way most adults looked at me when meeting me for the first time – with a look of uncertainty. My unfiltered words constantly caused moments of silence.

"Thanks," Stew said. "Let me call Cilantra's mom and let her know you girls arrived safely."

"Wait," Cilantra replied with a raised eyebrow. "My mom called here?"

"Yes. She looked up the number online from the address. She said she likes humoring her daughter's adventures, as long as she knows where you are." Stew seemed impressed with

Cilantra's mom's vigilance. "She also said you can call her if you need a ride home."

Then Stew said, "Follow me to the living room. I think you'll enjoy talking to my mom. She's really funny and direct, like you, Josie."

We entered the living room, where an old lady was sitting on a flower couch. The room was bright, with big windows and only white sheers to reflect the afternoon sunlight. There were two couches, one small and one large. In the center of the room was a circular ottoman with a large wooden serving tray, with what looked like three tall glasses of lemonade.

"I would get up and greet you young ladies, but my hip is hurting. Please have a seat." Maxime motioned to the couch at an angle to hers. Cilantra and I sat next to each other. I could smell the sweat from her palms. Or maybe those were my palms. I was sweating a lot from the walk.

Stew clapped his hands together and said, "I'll be in the office doing some paperwork. Let me know if you need anything. We have lots of cookies and milk if kids still like those kinds of things." With that, he exited the living room.

"Stew is trying to convince me to sell the house. He wants me to move in with him and his daughter. His wife passed away several years ago. He's a good boy." She looked at the serving tray. "I made you some freshly squeezed lemonade. I hope you don't mind."

"Not at all," I said as I reached for one of the cool glasses.

Cilantra reached for hers too and began to speak.

"Like I said on the phone, my name is Cilantra, and this is my best friend, Josie. We live in Carrington, right down the street." She paused and made sure Maxime was listening. When Maxime nodded her head, Cilantra continued.

"We're here because we were researching supernatural history from this town and yours was one of the stories in a book." She pulled off her backpack and unzipped it. She removed the history book and set it on the table.

Maxime smiled and said, "Yes, I have a copy of that book."

"We've read your story like 20 times!" I gushed. Maxime laughed.

"We read your story because we experienced something similar, right here in Langdon field. Josie saw a singing bird at night, and it was glowing. And she has a special rock."

At the mention of the rock, Maxime's face brightened. "What do you mean, special?"

I stood up and reached into my pocket. I removed the rock and saw that the etchings had a faint glow.

"Wow!" I said to the room. "It hasn't done that in months."

Maxime held out her hand and said, "May I?"

"Sure." I placed the rock in her hand.

"Tell me about it, please."

I scratched my head and said with honesty, "I'm not really sure where to start. Um, my dog found it in an empty lot, where it was glowing. I took it home, and that night I dreamt of a rainbow path. I followed the path and saw the future, where Cilantra was being chased by evil men. That was before I met her. She escaped and then police officers visited our home."

Maxime gasped a little and I stopped talking to hear what she had to say.

"Well, you read my story in the book, so I'll skip the long version. One of the officers from that night gave me the yellow rock. It was hot to the touch. At first, I wasn't sure if I wanted it. I put it in my purse, and they gave me a ride home since my car was totaled. All I wanted to do was go to sleep and forget about the incident. Besides, I was worried about vehicle repairs.

I was living at home with my parents at the time. When they saw me pull up into the driveway in a cop car, they were concerned. We spent several hours trying to figure out the car situation. By the time I went to bed, it was late, and I was exhausted. I forgot about the rock until about two or three in the morning when my room was lit with a bright light. I sat up in bed, startled, and began searching for the source of the light. I noticed my purse was glowing the most, so I made my way to it and then felt around inside. The yellow rock was the source, and it was very hot to the touch. But it was odd because it wasn't burning a hole in my purse or the table.

As I searched the room for an object I could pick the rock up with, I noticed one of the walls was transparent, as though made of glass. I thought to myself, 'That can't be right.' I stepped closer to the wall and saw the boathouse as clear as day. I remember pinching myself and wondering if I was in a dream.

Just then there was a knock on my door, and I jumped back into bed. The room went back to normal just as my dad entered and asked why all the lights were on. Even as an adult, I still had the fear of God for my parents. I blurted out that I found a glowing rock, and it lit up my room. My dad yawned and told me to be more considerate for those who work in the morning. At the time, I was only working in the afternoons and attending university in the mornings.

After that night, the yellow rock remained silent. I researched and found Kelsey, but she didn't want anything to do with the supernatural. I felt alone and decided I wouldn't pursue it any further. I still have the yellow rock. I kept it in a jewelry box that my mother gave me." She reached around behind her and produced a small, gold jewelry box, with a mirror on top. She handed it to Cilantra and said, "I decided, after speaking with you this morning, that I would give it to you girls. Nobody else can appreciate it the way you do."

"Wow, Maxime! Thank you so much." Cilantra took possession of the box and opened it. Inside was a dim yellow rock, with an etching of a unicorn.

"Yes," said Maxime. "I am an elderly woman, and my time on this earth is probably nearing its end. I have one son, and he seems to have outgrown his imagination. And his daughter is more interested in cell phones and tablets than talisman objects."

There was that word again. "Maxime, sorry to interrupt. What's a talisman? The first time I heard that word I thought it was pronounced 'tall man'?"

Maxime chuckled a little and said, "A talisman is an object with supernatural connections or powers. That's the best way I can explain it."

"Makes sense," I said.

Cilantra made the next inquiry. "Maxime, when you researched, did you ever figure out the unicorn drawing on the side of the rock? Like, I wonder if unicorns were really ancient magical animals."

"Yes. I researched unicorns but didn't find one with those kinds of embellishments." She pointed at the arrow design on the unicorn's neck. She continued, "Maybe with all of the internet nowadays, you gals can find some answers."

We sat in the living room for another hour and talked about ancient folklore and supernatural TV shows. I looked at my phone and realized the battery power was down to 2%. My mom was going to give me a tongue lashing. I elbowed Cilantra and said gently, "My phone battery is dying. We should probably head back."

Maxime smiled and put her hand to her chin, as though considering something important.

"I don't know you girls, but something tells me that you'll look for a lot of answers and adventures. Promise me that you will be careful and give your parents some credit. I wish I would have been more open with my parents about the yellow rock. When seeking supernatural answers, sometimes strange paths open up."

"I don't understand," I said.

Maxime responded with, "Just be careful. These days there are too many criminals trying to take advantage of young individuals such as yourselves. Cilantra, you've already been targeted and should be extra cautious."

"Yes, ma'am." Cilantra quietly agreed.

"You girls enjoy the rest of the day. You are welcome to return and speak with me or introduce me to your parents at any time."

"My parents would like that," I said.

Maxime responded, "Very good."

"Also, on the way out, can you please send Stew in here? I'll need his help sitting outside."

"Of course." Cilantra stood up and put the jewelry box into her backpack.

I waited for Cilantra to finish loading up, and then we exited the room together. Instead of going left, we went right and walked into the study, where Stew was in front of the computer.

"Hey Stew, your mom says she needs help sitting outside. We're leaving now or our parents will be worried."

Stew swiveled in his chair and said, "Okay. Cilantra, I'll call your mom and let her know you guys are walking back." He stood up from his chair and followed us into the hallway.

We walked to the front door then I turned around and said, "Your mom is really cool for an old lady."

Stew laughed, "Yea, I'll tell her you think so."

We exited the front door and began our walk the same way we came. The garden smelled delicious at this time of day. If Cilantra didn't have to be home, I would have wandered along the path and picked a few flowers for our dining table.

On the way back, we walked a little closer to the boathouse. We were speaking in excited tones and not paying attention to our surroundings. It was still daylight outside, and our sense of security was intact because the sun was shining. From behind a tall shrub, a hand shot out and grabbed Cilantra. The same man from the van stood up and covered her mouth while dragging her to the side of the boathouse. I was shocked and immediately started screaming. Thirty seconds later, I saw two men on the other side of the boathouse, holding Cilantra inside a small powerboat. It was already propelling its way to the distant shoreline.

Shocked, I fumbled for my phone and saw the battery was dead. I screamed Cilantra's name, too frozen to do anything else. Horrified, I finally found my strength and grabbed Cilantra's backpack. She must have dropped it during the quick struggle. I knew Cilantra's phone was in the front pocket. With trembling hands, I pulled it out and dialed 911.

"911 what is your emergency?" the dispatcher said.

"My friend's been kidnapped. I'm near the historic boathouse, in Carrington. Hurry! The men are in a boat."

As I was speaking to the operator, I could hear Stew's voice from half a block away, "Mom!"

Chapter 13

It was one of the longest nights of my life. There were police, detectives, camera crews, ambulances, and hysterical family members. Within the span of five minutes, our lives had gone from normal to abnormal. I had seen documentaries about this kind of stuff, but I wasn't prepared for the aftermath of shock.

Cilantra's mom was clinging to her husband, who was doing his best just to remain standing. My parents were sobbing. They were so shaken that they couldn't decide if they were going to yell at me about my inoperable cell phone, or if they were just going to comfort me. They were really upset as they listened to the details of the two men who were hiding behind the boathouse. And they were upset with themselves because they realized how little they knew of our Langdon field research.

Officer Ray walked up to where we were huddled and, with a sullen voice, told us to go back home and wait for their call. I was hesitant to leave Cilantra's parents, but it seemed like the detectives had everything under control. In addition to the abduction, the police were also dealing with a dead Maxime. She was found with an arrow protruding from her body, where it entered her heart, and the tip exited the back.

She died instantly, sitting in her blue plastic chair, facing the water.

Her son had heard my screams and walked outside to investigate. He found his mother slumped in her chair. He noticed the small boat heading north in the canal.

The police arrived five minutes after the phone call, and everything else felt too surreal.

It was a quiet car ride back to our home. We pulled up into the driveway and sat in the car, waiting for someone to speak. My dad broke the silence, "Josie, I want you to sleep in the master bedroom tonight. Your mom will sleep in the bed with you, and I am going to sleep on the couch if I sleep at all." He let out a deep sigh, "Tomorrow, we are going to have a family meeting. No more secrets."

"Yes, sir," I said.

"The two of you stay here in the car, while I check the house. I'll wave you guys in as soon as I've made sure all the windows and doors are locked. Then you guys can come inside. I'll walk Zeke around the outside of the house and make sure all the floodlights are working."

"Oliver," my mom said. "There's a baseball bat in the garage. Please be safe and take my whistle. Blow on it if there's someone in the house. And we'll honk the horn if we see something outside."

"All right," Dad said. He opened the car door and walked to the front porch, where his silhouette looked tired and slouched. I could hear Zeke barking inside as my dad put the key into the lock. There was a sliver of light illuminating the grass, and then he entered the house and closed the door.

My mom turned and looked at me with concern, "Josie, if you remember anything else from tonight then you wake me up and tell me. Together, we'll call the police and help Cilantra's family as much as we can. Okay?"

I gulped and held back another barrage of tears. "Yes," I chirped.

It seemed like ages passed before my dad reappeared at the front porch, this time with Zeke on a leash. He waved at us, giving the signal to enter our home. We exited the car and made haste to the front hallway. Dad closed the front door, and then walked with Zeke around the perimeter.

Suddenly, I felt as though my legs were like paper mâché. My knees buckled, and I reached out in front of me before collapsing onto the stairway landing. From the corner of my eyes, I saw my mom shouting my name, but I couldn't hear her. Then everything went blurry.

I woke up in my parents' bed about two minutes later, with my dad standing above me and leaning toward my face with a wet towel. I smiled and reached for his neck. He scooped me up into a sitting position and said, "Your body is processing shock. A few more minutes, and we would've called an ambulance."

My mom was sitting next to me and squeezed my hand. "I'm here, sweetie. Just sleep, and let us take care of the rest."

"Okay, Mom. I'm so sad. But I'll sleep. Can you send Zeke in here?"

My dad went to the doorway and called out Zeke's name. He came running up the stairs and into the bedroom. I patted the bed, and he jumped up and licked my face. I pulled him in close to me then closed my eyes and woke up the next morning.

Chapter 14

Sometime after sunrise, the phone rang. I couldn't hear the conversation from upstairs, but I could hear my dad's reaction. He cleared his throat and said, "I'm so sorry. If there is anything we can do to help, please call us. We'll be speaking to Josie this morning to find out if there are any more details. They will catch them."

My dad hung up the phone and began crying. My mom ran downstairs, and I heard her speak to him in slow, whispered tones. He responded with two quick phrases, and then my mom started crying. It was more than I could bear. I slowly made my way down the steps and entered the kitchen. Mom and Dad looked at me and said nothing.

"Josie, your dad and I need to talk for a few minutes. Why don't you go upstairs and wait in your room?"

Without a word, I exited the kitchen and walked up the stairs. My stomach was in knots, and my fists were clenched. If Cilantra was dead, then I would lock myself in my room until the world disappeared.

I went into my bedroom and stood at the window, trying to remember the rainbow path that led up and then straight across the street. Zeke was my only real friend then until I met

Cilantra. Even though she was younger than me, I could relate to her. She was funny and smart, and we both realized our special abilities. Maybe we should've spoken to our parents about the supernatural stuff, but it was also fun just having somebody who understood me.

I heard a knock at my bedroom door. "Josie, sit down, please." My mother's face looked ancient. She was holding my dad's hand for support.

"Your father and I have something to tell you. We were trying to decide whether or not we would talk about everything, but I think it's important you know the truth so you can protect yourself. And of course, we will protect you too."

I sat on my bed just as I was starting to see pins and needles in my vision, and I could feel my equilibrium shift.

My mom continued, "The police found Cilantra's body this morning. She was strangled and put into a tarp, near an abandoned field." My mom cleared her throat, and her voice quivered as she spoke, "She was also raped."

"I thought raped and strangled were the same thing?" I asked.

"Lord, I can't do this." My mom stood up and rubbed her palms onto the sides of her jeans.

"No." My mom took a deep breath, looked me in the eyes, and said as quickly and as matter-of-fact as possible, "Rape is not the same as strangling. Rape is a sexual crime. Do you remember our talk about sexual intercourse?"

"Yes." I gulped, remembering how my mom reenacted sexual relations with Barbie dolls to reiterate the explanation. She was embarrassed then, just like she was embarrassed now.

"Well, rape is forced sexual intercourse. Because, with sex, two people can decide to be intimate together. The male can put his penis in the female's vagina, with permission." She squeezed my dad's hand again and then continued. "Rape is the opposite. It's when the male or female forces intimacy, or forces the penis into the vagina, without permission."

Tears were streaming from my dad's eyes. He jumped in and said, "I think that's enough, sweetie." He squeezed her hand indicating that she should stop. Especially, since there was probably a terrified expression on my face. My dad attempted to smooth the conversation. "We've spoken about sex before and how two people who are experiencing love have intimacy. That's how babies are born. Well, uh… sometimes, that same experience happens if there isn't love, and there isn't mutual permission, and people can be hurt."

"Somebody forced a penis inside Cilantra and hurt her?" I asked.

"Yes, well, no. I don't know," my mom said.

"But they killed her. They choked her. She was probably fighting against them." I started crying uncontrollably. The visual of two men attacking my best friend was too much. Why didn't I chase them and jump into the boat? The two of us could have fought them together, or I could have dragged her from the boat. There were so many things I could have done instead of standing there and screaming.

I grabbed a fistful of my hair and ripped it out. Then I punched myself in the face until my dad grabbed my hands and threw himself on top of me. I screamed at the top of my lungs and then screamed and screamed until I felt like my tonsils would implode. I gasped for air and kept screaming.

My mom sat on the floor and leaned against the nightstand, allowing the sobs to overtake her composure. She covered her ears with her hands. Zeke was watching the chaos unfold and did not know which way to go. He licked my mom's tears and then jumped onto the bed and started barking at me. I could not stop screaming.

My dad picked me up out of the bed and ran with me down the stairs and outside. He put me in the backseat of his car and then jumped into the driver seat. I was still screaming as he backed out of the driveway.

Chapter 15

Ten minutes later, we arrived at the hospital, where my dad parked in front, pulled me out, and left the engine running. The screaming scared everybody inside the emergency room. My dad yelled, "We need a Doctor now!" A nurse ran from behind the reception desk and escorted us to the back area. "Sir, why is she screaming?" she shouted as she ushered us into a private room. My dad sat me on the screening table and then motioned for the nurse to follow him outside. They exited the room and shut the door. I could still hear what they were saying as I was gasping for air to fill my heated lungs. "She's my daughter, she has Down Syndrome, and she's just experienced her best friend's death. She is in shock." The nurse covered her own mouth and said, "Let me get the Doctor right away."

My throat was finally dry, and my screams were sounding raspy. But I kept going because if I was not screaming then I would have to deal with Cilantra's death. The Doctor entered the room, grabbed my hand, and gave it a gentle squeeze.

"Josie, I want you to keep screaming. I want you to know that it's okay to scream the pain away. And if you want, I can give you a sleeping pill so that you can relax here in this room and give your body a chance to heal." The Doctor looked at me with kindness.

I stopped screaming and started crying. The Doctor hugged me and said, "I'm Doctor George. Your dad here is really worried about you. Would you like to talk to him alone in the room while I see if I can find a sleeping pill?"

I nodded yes and then stopped crying. The thought of a sleeping pill to help me forget about my broken heart sounded like the most I could hope for if I stood a chance at any kind of normality. The nurse stepped in to hold my hand as the Doctor stepped out of the room. My dad rubbed my head and said, "I need to call home and make sure your mom is all right. She doesn't know we're here." He pulled out his cell phone and called our home from the room. My mom answered at the first ring and sounded frightened. I could hear her telling him that somebody tried breaking into the house, just moments after we left in the car. She dialed 911 and said the police were on their way.

Just then I remembered the backpack. I tried yelling at the phone, but my voice cracked. I said in a hoarse whisper, "They want the backpack." My dad repeated what I said, and my mom asked if it was the backpack I had with me last night. I nodded yes and said it was Cilantra's backpack. My dad's eyes widened, and he described what I mentioned. He hung up the phone and said Mom was going to investigate and let the police know as soon as they showed up.

The Doctor returned to the room, holding a small blue plastic cup. He reached into his pocket and pulled out a pill. "Dad, if you're okay with a sleeping pill I'll need you to sign some forms. We'll sedate her and let her sleep the shock away. We'll start an I.V. to make sure she stays hydrated. We've paged the on-call pediatric psychiatrist who should be here soon."

"Doc," my dad said. "I could use one of those myself."

"We are going to admit her to the hospital, where she'll have her own room and a place for guests to sleep. The psychiatrist will speak with you this evening to get a better sense of what's going on and then they'll be back early tomorrow to speak with Josie."

"Sounds good." My dad gestured to the pill and said, "That's not addictive is it?"

"Not at all," the Doctor replied. He then put the pill into my palm and handed me the cup of water. "Go ahead, Josie. Take the pill and go to sleep. We can move this bed into the hospital room."

My dad walked over to me and kissed my cheek. I swallowed the pill and drank the water. Within minutes, my eyelids felt heavy and the room gently drifted into a haze of light and soft voices.

Chapter 16

The next morning, my eyes fluttered open just as my stomach was gurgling. Our current room was much larger than the room from last night. I guess they moved my bed. My mom was asleep in the second bed, and my dad was snoring in a reclining chair. My throat felt dry, like sandpaper on my tonsils. To my right, the window blinds were partially open, and gold streams of light were touching the corners of my comforter. Little flecks of dust were jumping and dancing, as though a spotlight were encouraging their flamboyant moves.

I wondered what it would be like, as a fleck of dust, flitting around and magnetically drawn to different surfaces. Would the universe pull me in like stardust? I thought about the first time I showed Cilantra how to operate a telescope. My dad showed me the complicated knobs and how to operate them and focus on particular stars. Cilantra laughed and danced around the telescope the first time she saw the Little Dipper. That was the night the hummingbird appeared in my room, while Cilantra was sleeping at my house. Cilantra was awakened from her slumber and saw the bird first. She threw one of my oranges at me to wake me up.

I woke up just as Zeke jumped onto the bed, barked once, and then lowered his head, as though he were bowing in the bird's direction. I rubbed my eyes and spoke, "Where's the portal? Cilantra says she doesn't know where the opening is, or how to close it." I realized my words were probably a little too harsh and added, "We found the rock."

The hummingbird sat in silence staring at Cilantra. When it spoke, it said something I didn't understand at the time.

"Cilantra, I'll be waiting."

Chapter 17

My dad's snoring woke him up. He sputtered what sounded like the phrase, 'in a pear tree.' I smiled because he had been obsessing about our holiday vacation before Cilantra's tragedy. Our plan was to spend Christmas at a bungalow, in St. Thomas Islands. He and my mom saved up enough money to book a huge suite at a fancy schmancy hotel. We were going to bring Zeke, but Cilantra's family had agreed to watch him during our time away from home.

The thought of Cilantra made my eyes sting with tears. I thought it was weird how everybody else tried to pretend as though they weren't crying, even in the most appropriate moments. Usually, if I cried, it was an instant flow of saltwater and boogers. This was one of those times where the emotions were too powerful to try and hide.

My dad heard the sniffles and sat up in the recliner. His hair was pointed in different directions, but his mind was sharp. He knew I was sad and crawled into my bed to comfort me. He wiped the tears from my eyes and pushed my bangs from my forehead, where he planted a sloppy kiss.

"Mom's still asleep. You want me to wake her?" he asked with a concerned look on his face.

I shook my head no and then wrapped my arms around his neck. He smelled like our garage, but with a lingering scent of lavender, from our garden. Sometimes, he would work on the front yard garden and then disappear into the garage, where he would repair antique furniture. He said it reminded him of his great-uncle, who owned a little antique furniture store. His uncle passed away years ago and left him some of his most treasured items.

My dad whispered in my ear, "Sweetie, I'm so sorry. I'm not sure if it was too soon to tell you the truth about Cilantra." He waited for my reaction. When there wasn't one, he continued. "I spoke with a Doctor about how strong you are and how we never really gave it a second thought to hold back because of the Down Syndrome. But maybe we just know you so well that we figured you could handle it. Was that a bad assumption?"

"I don't know." I let go of his neck and leaned back into the pile of pillows. "Some things about this world still scare me, like the first ten seconds after I walk into a cave and don't know what to expect," I confided. "But what you described about Cilantra's death was like a nightmare. I would rather hear it from you, than from the news. It's just… well… talking about sexual stuff is embarrassing. Talking about sexual stuff with parents is really embarrassing. And it was hard to understand what you were telling me about Cilantra. All I understood was that she possibly suffered."

My dad sighed a long, heavy sigh and took my hand. "Wouldn't it be really cliché if I just let your mom speak with you? I always hear about dads who pawn the sex conversations onto the moms. And since this happened to someone you know, I felt like I should at least attempt a serious conversation."

"I understand," I whispered.

My dad looked me in the eyes to make sure I wasn't just saying that to make him stop talking.

"If you want, the Doctor is going to speak with you today. She wants to make sure you can process the information in a way that doesn't cause more shock. Is that okay with you?"

"Dad, I feel like I should be helping the police find Cilantra's killers. There's so much that Cilantra and I were keeping from you and her parents too. Maybe after we find the bad guys, then we can talk about the stuff that makes me uncomfortable." I glanced at him to make sure I wasn't hurting his feelings.

Now it was his turn. "I understand," he said. "Why don't we wake your mom up and then you can tell both of us what you've been hiding from us. Then your mom and I can talk and decide if it's information that should be shared with the police."

Just then, a nurse entered the room with a clipboard. She smiled and made her way over to my bed.

"How are we feeling today?" she asked.

"Like a little alien clawed at my tonsils, then pinched my eyelids to make them look swollen." I managed a small smile.

"Is he still here? Because if he is, I'll poke his tonsils with my stethoscope." She held up her stethoscope to reiterate her point.

My mom started to move in the bed, at the sound of our raised voices. She slowly sat up and groggily greeted the nurse. She looked at me and said, "Hi sweetie. I love you so much."

The nurse chimed in and reassured my parents. "I'm just here to get a read on Josie's vitals. Give me two minutes and then I'll let the Doctor know everyone's awake."

"Actually, when you have the vitals, could you give us the room for about an hour? We need to have a family discussion," said my mom in a clear tone, her previous grogginess gone.

The nurse nodded and said, "Yes, of course, and I'll make sure none of the other nurses disturb you."

"Thanks," my dad said.

With that, the nurse tended to my vitals and jotted down some notes on her clipboard. She exited the room, with a quick glance at the three of us and closed the door softly.

Chapter 18

My mom swung her legs over the side of the bed and paused before gently pushing herself up. She looked at me and pressed her lips together, as though attempting a sad smile.

"Let me brush my teeth and freshen up, then we'll talk." After she walked into the restroom, I was aware of the dryness of my mouth and throat. I reached for the bottle of water sitting on the nightstand next to the bed, grabbed it, and chugged until the water was dripping down my chin.

My dad stood up and lifted his arms to smell his armpits, then he put his hand in his pocket and pulled out a packet of gum. "Want one?" he asked.

"Yes, please," I said and extended my hand. He put the small rectangle of juicy goodness into my hand and then unwrapped his and placed it in his mouth. The smell of super sweet cherry made my mouth water. It reminded me of the first bite of homemade cherry pie, which my mom used to make for Thanksgiving. Now, my dad actually purchased pies from a local celebrity – a chef with her own TV show. He said it was a good way to show support for the community and make lasting business relationships. The cherry-flavored gum was a welcome variation.

As I was chomping on the tender gooiness, my mom exited the restroom and made her way to my bed. She hugged and kissed my dad and then squeezed my hand. My dad said, "Excuse me, give me five minutes in the restroom, and then we'll have our family meeting."

My mom sat at the edge of the hospital bed and asked, "How are you feeling?"

"Numb," I responded.

"I'm sorry, Josie. I feel like we put too much on you. Like it was too much to hear about a friend dying and then to hear how she died." My mom's eyes watered, and she looked at the opposite wall.

"Mom, how is it possible that someone could enter my life unexpectedly, become my closest friend, and then be gone so suddenly? I feel like a memory foam pillow. Like I fit myself around her life, and now I'm just waiting for time to bounce me back to my old life."

My mom looked at me with astonishment. "Sometimes you say the wisest things," she said.

"Really?" I asked.

"Seriously. Like, remember the time cousin Sam's turtle died, and you told him his soul was ancient and would pass on to the next generation of little turtles?"

I smiled at remembering Sam's response. He said he would catch a bunch of baby turtles and name them after his deceased turtle.

My mom continued, "I've always said there's so little we know about your extra chromosome. It's like that one little DNA strand holds nuggets of wisdom and lots of love."

"I don't know where I come up with the stuff I say sometimes," I said.

Right on cue, my dad exited the restroom and said, "Let's talk and then figure out the logistics of next steps. I called the office and told them I would be out today."

"I'll start. There's a lot I wanted to say, but I wasn't sure if you guys would believe me. I hardly believe it myself, but having Cilantra around was a huge piece of the puzzle."

I spent the next ten minutes telling them about Zeke finding the glowing rock, the arm reaching down from the middle of the air, the dream with the rainbow path and alternate dimension, the vision of the girl with the purple coat, the hummingbird, the dancing zipper, the supernatural history book, the mission to close the portal above our town, and the visit with Maxime. They asked me to clarify a few things, but they seemed to understand. They raised their eyebrows every now and again, in a 'did she just say that' kind of way.

My mom breathed a sigh of relief and said, "I'm glad you guys weren't doing anything illegal." She stood up and walked to the far side of the second bed, where she lifted Cilantra's backpack. "I have Cilantra's backpack. We'll do a quick search and then provide the backpack to the Investigators."

Dad said, "I've seen my fair share of Star Trek and sci-fi movies. Somehow, that makes it harder for me to believe that any of this stuff is real. Why is it always the children who can see the supernatural? My earliest memories are from a bus ride in kindergarten, then a few more memories in third grade. Did I encounter supernatural when I was a kid and then block it out?"

My mom responded, "When I was growing up, we always went to church and heard stories about supernatural healings. At the time, we thought it was just normal. And then I became an adult and those kinds of experiences seemed more distant."

My dad said, "I want to believe. And for the sake of keeping Cilantra's memory alive, I'm all in. But is this information that her parents would want to know, or would they think we're crazy?"

"As far as I know, Cilantra never spoke to her parents about our adventures. But she said her mom was really open to spiritual books," I said.

"Then, let's do our own investigation, and we'll wait until after the funeral to approach her parents," my mom responded.

"My engineer mind wants to analyze and organize, so let me just speak aloud what I'm thinking, and you guys tell me if you agree." My dad scratched his chin and continued, "Josie, if what you're saying is true, then our town is a portal. We don't know where the portal leads to or how it opens. There are at least two bad men, from unknown origins, who are attempting to control the portal. We don't know who they are, or what they want. Their first target, that we know of, was Cilantra."

"And the two rocks and zipper are some kind of talisman, leading to the portal," my mom chimed in.

"Right," my dad said. "But we don't know how they work."

"If we show the objects to the police, then they'll think we're nuts. They would be less than thrilled if we told them there are dimensional killers on the loose. I might as well waltz into the police station with a stack of comic books and tell them those are recorded history of my home planet." My dad scratched the back of his head.

"Josie, does the magic rock glow only if a rainbow portal is getting ready to open up?" My mom looked at the rock sitting on the bed.

"Um, yes. Now that you mention it, that seems to be the only time it's glowed," I said.

"Is there anything else in common that would link the rock glowing and the portal opening? Like a thunderstorm, or a certain time of night?"

"I'm not sure what time of day the portal appears," I confessed.

"But now that we have two magic stones, maybe they'll function together?" My dad sounded hopeful. "We didn't get a chance to tell you, but last night, there was an attempted break-in at our home. Your mother heard one of the back doors rattling and went to investigate, probably about ten minutes after we left for the hospital. She saw a movement in the trees between our yard and the neighbor's yard and called the cops. One of the investigators was Officer Ray, who's been involved with protecting Cilantra since the first attempted kidnapping.

"He said it looked like somebody tried to pry the doors open with a crowbar. The wood around the door splintered. He was really concerned and drove your mom to the hospital. He and his partner patrolled the neighborhood last night but didn't see anything. At the time, we didn't understand why they would try to enter our house so soon after a murder. If it's the same guys, then they really risked their lives to try and enter our home. Maybe it's the stones they're looking for?" My dad's voice seemed to raise an octave as he realized he was piecing together a puzzle.

"That makes sense," I said.

"Here's what we should do today, to make the most of our time, help solve Cilantra's murder and close a portal… Maybe not all at once, but to take steps in the correct direction." My mom pushed up her sleeves and continued speaking.

"Josie, you and I are going to stay here and speak with the Doctor about how to deal with Cilantra's murder. I think it's important that we don't jump into solving a mystery just so we can avoid the sadness. While you and I are here, your dad is going to go back to our home, with the backpack.

"Oliver, I want you to look around Josie's room for clues about how and when the rocks might do their magic stuff again. Then, visit with Cilantra's parents. Tell them Josie and I will pay them a visit as soon as Josie is feeling better. Ask them if Cilantra ever spoke to them about supernatural themes. Tell them we're not sure how the girls' interests might have attracted the perps, but we're trying to remember as much detail as possible. Let them know they can call us any time of day or night, and we're here to help solve as much as we can."

My dad sighed, "That's a tall order, but I think I can manage."

"And don't forget to walk and feed Zeke. We should be home around four or five. I'll call Uber and pick up some carry out and maybe make a quick grocery store visit. We'll return home, prep dinner and segue into the living room to read the supernatural history book together. Tonight, we'll all sleep in Josie's room, and maybe, just maybe the portal will open." My mom shrugged her shoulders, knowing that making all these plans would not necessarily lead to a dimension jump. Although, I was impressed with how quickly she developed our next steps.

My dad stood up and gathered his wallet and car keys. He put those and the two rocks into the backpack, then he paused and said, "I'll head home now and then I'll call you when I'm on my way to Cilantra's place." He leaned in and planted a kiss on my mom's cheek. "You ladies are the loves of my life. No matter what we uncover, we will persevere together." With that, he picked up the backpack and walked out of the hospital room with a mission.

Chapter 19

My mom and I met with the Pediatric Psychologist. Her name was Beverly, and she was the mother of a young autistic son and two older children. She understood how to communicate and how to make me communicate. I told Beverly that Cilantra and I were best friends and that I had a premonition something would happen to her. That seemed to be more of an easy explanation than talking about magic hummingbirds.

"Josie, you're like the coolest kid I've ever met. You understand my role, and you're totally willing to help me help you. Does that make sense?"

"Yes, it does," I said.

"I think the hardest part of recovering from Cilantra's death is knowing the details about how she was murdered. It would be easier to digest if your mom said, 'she died from shock.' Instead, your parents were brave and decided not to hold anything back. They gave you the benefit of the doubt, and you showed them how capable you are of processing information."

"Beverly, I screamed for two hours. I don't remember much of our conversation," I said.

"It's better that you screamed, rather than ignore the tragedy. There is nothing wrong with screaming in the right circumstance." She placed her hand under her chin and thought about what she wanted to say next.

"Here's what I want you to do – close your eyes and tell me the first memory that comes to mind of you and Cilantra." Beverly smiled, and her dimples made her eyes look ten times brighter.

I closed my eyes and focused on Cilantra's face. The first memory that drifted up was when she and I were having a slumber party in my room. We were lying on the floor, on our backs, with our feet resting on the edge of the bed. Cilantra said we should try to interlace our toes. We tried for two hours to wiggle our big toe between the other's second toe and so on. Every time our feet started sweating it was difficult to keep a grip. We laughed until our bellies hurt. Zeke kept jumping onto the bed to try and lick our feet, which made us laugh more.

The thought of our innocent laughter made me start crying. The stream started as droplets of tears and then morphed into sobs. My body heaved as though experiencing hiccups. It was like a dark density cloud was sitting on my chest. If sadness had weight, it would weigh about twelve ounces – like one of my water bottles, filled with tears.

Beverly sat next to me on the bed and put her arm around my shaking shoulders. "Those are the memories the bad guys can never take away." She cupped her hand under my chin and gradually, I looked into her eyes. "Hold on to those pleasant memories and eventually, the tears become frowns and the frowns become smiles."

I hugged Dr. Beverly and allowed myself to cry with a renewed sense of purpose to figure out Cilantra's mystery so that her death would be part of a hero's tale.

Chapter 20

My mom and I left the Doctor's office and went to the grocery store to pick up quick meals and restock the fridge. Dad called once and said he was on his way to Cilantra's home. While we were at the grocery store, I heard two of the neighbors talking about Cilantra's and Maxime's murders. They were speaking in whispered tones and with a sense of urgency.

The only phrase I could make out was, '…the arrow belonged to a museum.'

I walked up to the overweight lady with a shiny brown purse and said, "Sorry, sorry. I heard you speaking about the arrow from Maxime's home. I'm Cilantra's friend. Did you say it was from a museum?" I raised my eyebrows anticipating a response.

The second lady, who was wearing a scarf, pursed her lips and said, "We're speaking amongst ourselves, as adults. Where is your parent? This is a sensitive topic and you seem like somebody who would need adult supervision." She looked startled when my mom appeared and tapped me on the shoulder.

"Josie, go to the beverages section and grab some of those flavored ice teas, one for each of us." As she spoke, she maintained eye contact with the lady who proverbially shut me down. I was embarrassed because I knew my mom was getting ready to make a scene. Over the years, I learned that my mom would always be fiercely protective. The Down Syndrome never seemed like Down Syndrome to me, but my mom was aware of how society treated me, whether good or bad.

I made my way to the beverages area and found the section with cold iced teas. There were so many flavors to choose from, but I usually always selected mango and vanilla. As I was reaching for the bottles, I could hear both ladies reacting to whatever my mom said. There were the usual responses of, 'Well! I never…' and 'You can't talk to me like that.' Before they could utter another word, my mom swiveled on the heel of her foot and made a beeline for where I was standing. I could see her smirking a little and hoped no one else was watching.

"Come on, let's pay for this stuff and get out of here." She held out the basket so I could put the iced teas in, although there was barely any room.

"I have the essentials so you can stay home the next few days. Where should we pick up carryout food?" She ran her fingers through my hair and started walking back up the aisle.

"*Chic-Fil-A*," I said with no hesitation. I was craving their deluxe sandwiches.

Chapter 21

We made it home and found the house empty. My dad had taken Zeke to Cilantra's place, probably to make sure he wasn't cooped up for long periods of time.

"Josie, why don't you go upstairs and thoroughly clean your room? Vacuum, dust, polish, do some laundry, and wash the sheets. Make your room comfortable so dad and I can fit for our sleepover."

"Yes, ma'am." I smiled and rummaged in the shopping bag until I found the vanilla iced tea.

Once upstairs, I breathed and let out a deep, heavy groan. I could feel the tingling in my nose, as my eyes brimmed with tears. The reality of Cilantra's absence from this world was depressing. I could only imagine what her parents must be going through, thinking about their child's death. I rubbed my face and inhaled the stale air from my room. There was a slight citrus scent, from the oranges on my desk.

I started with removing the bed comforter, pillow covers, and sheets. Those would take a while to wash, as well as the mound of clothes sitting in my closet. I noticed my dad had been at my desk, searching for something. The oranges were shifted to the left side of the surface, and there were papers sitting under the desk lamp. At first, the papers looked like drawings or lots of doodles. Upon further inspection, I realized the top page was a sketch of a bird. A hummingbird. Did I draw that? I slowly and gently traced the outline with my finger. Odd. I was sure that wasn't my drawing. Maybe Cilantra brought it over to one of our slumber parties. Sure enough, the lower right corner of the paper contained her signature.

I sat down in the chair and thought about when she could have left it. I wasn't even sure if she had mentioned it and I forgot, or if it was something she hid for me to find later – like the vacation message under the kitchen table. One of the things that impressed me most about Cilantra was how ahead of her age she was. She was nine, but sometimes she said things that sounded like she was twenty. I asked her about it once and she shrugged it off, saying, "My dad is really smart. He uses big words around the house a lot."

I made a mental note to speak with my dad about the bird drawing. He should be returning home within the next hour, and I needed to clean and scrub away the sadness. Depression smelled like body grease, or maybe that was the smell of my adrenaline, from screaming so much.

Chapter 22

I was just removing items from the dryer when I heard my dad's keys in the front door. Thanks to the washer's quick cycle, most of my laundry was already done. The bed was made, the rug vacuumed, the curtain sheers fluffed and pulled away from the window. The room smelled like fresh cranberries and cinnamon. Even Zeke's bed looked vibrant and new.

I ran downstairs and into the kitchen, then halted in my tracks when I saw my dad's face. His eyes were puffy and swollen. His posture slouched, and he looked unsure of himself.

"Dad?"

He swallowed a huge lump in his throat but didn't speak. He extended his arm and motioned for me to come near him. I walked toward him, and he wrapped his arms around me with a fierce hug.

"I'm glad it wasn't you," was all he could mutter.

My mom stopped setting the table and embraced both of us. We stood that way for about twenty seconds, then released when Zeke started pawing at our legs, whining to be let in.

"I'm ready to jump in the shower. I'll be down for dinner in about 30 minutes." My dad squeezed my mom's hand and exited the kitchen.

"Josie, go ahead and fill the glasses with iced tea. I'll keep the food on the stove until dad is out of the shower. I need to walk around the house and make sure all the doors and windows are locked. I forgot to check when we got home."

"Okay, Mom." I went to the fridge and pulled the iced teas out. I could sense tension, as I filled the glasses. Our house had never been this sad or felt as lonely before.

Mom reappeared a few minutes later. "All good! I think I'll go upstairs and see how dad's doing. Might put on my pajamas too."

"Okay, I'll watch the food," I said.

Chapter 23

Eventually, we all made it down to the dinner table. My dad looked like his normal self again, and he spoke with a purpose.

"Josie, tell me about the bird drawing in your room. Did you draw that?" he asked.

"No, I didn't. I was trying to remember if Cilantra drew it, gave it to me and I forgot, or if she hid it in my desk. How'd you find it?" I inquired.

"I don't know what prompted me to look. I only opened the top drawer of the desk, and there were a few sketches sitting on top of the notebooks." He inhaled another bite of his gyro.

"Cilantra must have left them then..." I looked down at my plate. It was hard thinking about our last interactions.

"Mom, I'm done eating. I'll take the book into the living room and wait for you guys." I picked up my plate and placed it into the sink. Although my stomach felt tight, I managed to eat most of the food. Instead of Chic-fil-A, we had gone to one of our favorite eateries, a traditional Greek restaurant. The meals were always fresh and full of interesting spices.

I walked into the entryway, where my dad had placed the supernatural history book onto the credenza. I thumbed through a few of its pages, wondering if he noted anything remarkable. The first page of Maxime's interview was dog-eared, and it looked like notes were scribbled into the margins. I didn't write inside the book, but it looked like my dad did. I lifted the book and carried it into the living room, where I plopped onto the far end of the couch; the leather sounded like a full water balloon.

I could hear a muffled conversation from the dining room. I really didn't feel like paying attention, as I'm sure my parents were probably trying to figure out how to speak with me about sensitive topics. There really wasn't much more to say. Two people had been murdered, one of them just so happened to be my best friend. The bigger issue was all the supernatural and unexplained mysteries surrounding their deaths, like the vortexes and the arrow. What if the portal opens tonight? Or what if it doesn't? Would my parents still believe? Just then, I realized how amazing my parents were and how willing they were to learn about stuff that most people would laugh at.

My parents entered the room together. They looked at me and then at each other before they took their usual seats. My dad always preferred the swanky recliner, with a cupholder and massager. My mom opted to sit at the opposite end of my favorite couch. She pulled the blanket from the ottoman and covered her legs.

My dad began the conversation with, "Cilantra's parents had a lot to say."

First, he described their reaction upon seeing him. He said Cilantra's dad opened the door, immediately hugged him and cried. The mother pulled them both into the house, which smelled like grief if grief had a smell. They sat in the living room, where my dad could hardly get a word in edgewise. The dad was rambling on about strange dreams and occurrences surrounding Cilantra's birth. He felt like he always knew she was chosen for something special. He said he didn't follow any particular religion, but that he was open to spirituality.

As a philologist, he spent time in Israel, studying the ancient Hebrew writings inscribed at various locations. For several years, he was fascinated with the bible's Jacob story and visited the supposed site where Jacob slept and had a vision of heaven. He said he felt drawn to that location and would've lived there permanently, with his wife, if his visa hadn't expired. It was shortly after his visit that he and his wife conceived a child.

He said he dreamt of Cilantra before she was named or born. He told his wife about the dream, and they sought the help of a Jewish scholar, who told them they should research Kabbala. At first, he didn't want to involve himself in religion, and then he figured speaking with a Rabbi might help explain his dreams. He humored himself and went to a local synagogue, where an old Rabbi teacher encouraged him to research his family history. The Rabbi and Cilantra's dad met every Sunday when most synagogues were closed. He taught Cilantra's dad the principles of the Jacob and Esau story and the importance of the hip injury representing a struggle with a divine being.

Cilantra's dad felt like he had unlocked something otherworldly in the area around Jacob's rock. Never had he ever had dreams, or at least, not that he could remember. He was sure the baby growing inside his wife's belly was tied to the whole experience. After a few months, the Rabbi and Cilantra's dad became close friends. Eventually, he showed

Cilantra's dad underground tunnels, where mysticism still literally ran deep.

When Cilantra was born, there was one night when the mother was asleep in the hospital bed and the baby in an incubator. The room was quiet, save for the nurses who he could hear on the opposite side of the door. As he was looking at Cilantra, he noticed a twinkling of light, just near her navel. He squinted, thinking he was seeing things, and just faintly made out a burst of pastel rainbow colors. The brilliant eruption only lasted a split second, but it was enough that he shot up in his chair, rubbed his eyes, and stared at his sleeping child. He thought for sure he must have imagined it. He knew he was sleep-deprived and chalked it up to weariness.

The first few months after Cilantra's birth were busy and exciting. Cilantra's dad didn't have a lot of time to meet with the Rabbi and continue his studies. And he confided in his wife that he was worried about some of the things the Rabbi was showing him, like light rituals, incantations, and certain talismans.

I stopped my dad and inquired again what a talisman was. My dad said it was an ordinary object or place that is either a powerful magical key or holds supernatural characteristics. I told them that Maxime and I had a similar conversation comparing the magical rocks to a talisman. My dad's eyes widened as he agreed, as though it were the first time he thought about the importance of the rocks.

Then, he continued to explain how over several years, Cilantra's dad soon forgot about Kabbala, until two months ago. He said the Rabbi paid him a visit and said he wanted to show him something. Intrigued, Cilantra's dad met with the Rabbi at his house. As he walked into the study, he noticed sketches covering the walls. The sketches were of his daughter, Cilantra, and one picture, the only one with color, showed a rainbow mist flowing from Cilantra's navel. Cilantra's dad was shocked and a little freaked out.

The Rabbi quickly explained how these were images from his dreams. He said he believed Cilantra was a living talisman, a portal into another dimension. He said he didn't want to meet her because he wanted to keep the dream details and revelations separate.

Cilantra's dad decided he would not divulge any of the information to his wife since she was already preoccupied with helping to raise their daughter. He also decided he would stop meeting with the Rabbi because he wasn't sure if he could raise a child in a religion he didn't understand. Not to mention, he often found himself staring at Cilantra, expecting the universe to open and reveal its secrets. How could he raise her as a normal child if all he ever did was revere her as a deity?

Of course, there were odd occurrences over the years, such as Cilantra appearing in different parts of the house at what would seem to be impossible speeds, if not for time and space disturbance. Then, there were the night terrors, when Cilantra would wake up screaming. She would tell him about two bad men who were chasing her outside. It was always the same dream, and she would wake up as soon as one of the bad guys grabbed the back of her shirt.

Cilantra's dad was now convinced that Cilantra experienced her death before it occurred. He said he only recently went into her room and found a large drawing of three pages with tape holding them together. The first page showed Cilantra walking, the second page showed Cilantra lying in a canoe, and the third page showed Cilantra jumping from the canoe into the body of a hummingbird. Almost as though the hummingbird had a pouch, like a kangaroo.

After Cilantra's dad stopped talking, my dad told him about the rocks and my experience with the rainbow dimension and the hummingbird. Cilantra's dad wept and asked himself why he never nurtured her spiritual talent. He was devastated and his wife was more of a mess because she realized how much Cilantra's dad had not been telling her. They were both appreciative of our open conversation and admired how much we were willing to help them. My dad made sure Cilantra's dad knew I would visit at the right time. They said they would understand if I didn't attend Cilantra's funeral services, but that they would like to meet with us a week from today.

"Here we are," said my dad as he motioned to the supernatural history book.

"Josie, why don't you read to us the stories from Carrington Field and let's see if any of the information is similar to what Cilantra's dad encountered."

"Sure," I said and picked up the book where the page tip was folded. I read both stories to them and could tell they were making connections. After I finished reading, my mom stood up and started pacing around the room.

"So, the rocks were talismen objects and Cilantra was guarding a portal. The portal opening is related to rainbows, and the portal itself is guarded by a talking hummingbird. Sounds like the makings of a science fiction movie," she said.

"And our mission is making the portal open, finding out who the bad guys are, where they're hiding, and how to close the portal for good," I responded.

"Not to mention, delivering the right amount of information to the police, in order to catch Cilantra's killers," my dad exclaimed.

"One thing that I am not understanding is why they killed Cilantra," my mom said. "Why not just kidnap her, access the portal, and then let her go?"

"Well, some cultures mistakenly believe that sex provides entrance to the soul or that sex with a minor somehow rids them of ailments." My dad shook his head as he spoke. "Maybe they felt like a violent death was the only way to find the portal opening. Either way, they need to be found and punished."

"I agree," I said. "They should be found and punished, but if I find them, then I'll make them suffer."

"Josie, absolutely not. We stick together and inform the police as soon as possible. These men are dangerous, and everything we do to help find them will be from a distance." The stern look on my mom's face told me she wasn't joking around.

Changing subjects, I said, "Dad, when you searched my room, did you find anything else that would explain how the rocks turned on?"

"No, I didn't. Although, I remember you saying there was a thunderstorm the first day of the portal opening, if that helps," he said.

"Hmmm, there's no thunderstorm tonight, but maybe with all of us sleeping in the same room, it'll open," my mom said. "Let's get ready for bed and then we'll join you in your room."

"All right," I said and lifted myself from the couch. Zeke followed at my heels as I made my way up the stairs.

Chapter 24

By ten p.m., we were all comfortably seated in my room. Mom and I were in my bed, dad was on the air mattress and Zeke was slumbering under the window. The room temperature was just right and soon we were dozing off while listening to nature's symphony outside my window.

I wasn't sure how long we were sleeping, but I was the first one to transition into the temporary dreamscape. I opened my eyes and saw the window sheers fluttering above my dad's head. Zeke was already standing at attention and wagging his tail, as though anticipating the portal opening. A few seconds later, the room filled with magnificent color and sparkles, which seemed to have a mind of their own and landed at my feet. I sprung out of bed and the glitter spread out around the room. I knew I needed to wake my parents up, but first I pinched myself. The sensation of pinched skin wasn't the same as in the real world. My nerves felt numb and gravity felt lighter as I walked from my side of the bed to my mom's side of the bed. I stood between my mom and dad before deciding to wake them up. They were sleeping so peacefully, but I knew they would be expecting this journey.

I gently tapped my mom's shoulder, and she immediately sat up in bed. She looked at me and said, "Is it happening? Are we there?" I laughed at her abruptness and nodded yes. Then, I walked toward my dad and poked my toe into his rib area. At first, he just swatted my foot away. I kept poking him until he finally sat up in the air mattress. He looked at my mom and me, then at Zeke. He said, "It's really bright in here, and there's so much glitter." He rubbed his eyes and then stood up from the mattress.

Suddenly, all three of the mysterious objects were glowing. The two rocks were sitting on the desk, glowing bright yellow and intense purple. The third item, the zipper, was sitting on the nightstand and pulsating a bright blue aura. It was also making a little chirping noise, like a subtle alarm clock. I picked it up and was surprised at how it maneuvered through the air, as though it were wearing a jet propulsion. It appeared it was attached to something on the other side of the air, something unseen. The zipper began to pull me toward the window, where a rainbow path was forming from the floor to the yard.

"The zipper is pulling me," I said.

"We're right beside you," my dad assured.

We continued together and walked through the wall and window. My mom was fascinated with the dreamscape environment. She was moving her hand in front of her face and staring at the way the sparkles danced above and around her. We continued walking for what seemed like mere seconds, but we arrived at Carrington Park, which was at least a mile from our house. There, in the middle of the field, flew the hummingbird. The sumptuous song sounds were drifting toward us with smooth elegance. We closed the distance between us with just a few steps. Mom and Dad were staring at the hummingbird with awe and amazement. Then, the hummingbird spoke and said, "I'm glad you're here."

I was still gripping the zipper and holding it out in front of me, or rather, it was holding me. The hummingbird gently touched the zipper with its beak, and I felt it lock into place, although there was nothing there that it was attached to.

"Open the portal," the hummingbird said.

I looked at the zipper and knew instinctively what to do. I pulled it down, in a vertical direction. There, before our very eyes, a doorway opened up. On the other side, we could see a different dimension. The hummingbird spoke and said, "All of us need to enter in a single line since the doorway is small."

I let go of the zipper, and my dad said, "Josie, I'll go first."

The hummingbird corrected him, "No, Josie goes first. I'm here. She's safe. Cilantra transferred the portal key to Josie. She needs to enter the alternate dimension first and seal the spiritual bridge."

My dad grabbed the back of my pajama top and said, "Then, let's go."

Chapter 25

I walked through the opening and immediately felt the temperature difference. It was dark outside, and it was hard to make out the surrounding area. There were lightning bugs everywhere! But their lights were different colors so that they looked like a symphony of colorful shooting stars.

My dad spoke, "This is awesome. What are we supposed to do here?"

"We have until sunrise, for me to teach you the basics of this dimension. Then, we locate the third stone. Once we have the third stone, we must hurry to the portal opening above Carrington Field. Only ten minutes have passed since all of you went to sleep. Keep the stones hidden and then I will instruct you how to seal one of the portals, to keep the Sashima men away."

"Sashima?" I asked.

"I will explain soon," said the hummingbird.

"Where should we go for five hours?" my mom whispered, as though the lightning bugs would be disturbed by the sound of our voices.

"We're going to the ruby forest. There's a large floating cabin, where we can transport ourselves to the area where the third stone has been hidden. The stone is probably guarded, so we'll need to come up with a distraction and a way to keep Josie safe."

"Tell us which direction to walk," my dad said. He was still looking at all the lightning bugs and attempting to catch them in his hands.

"There's a portal transport up ahead. We'll step in, then step out and quickly make our way to the cabin. Follow me." The hummingbird drifted gracefully to a glowing orange orb. She made a singing sound, and the portal expanded. Within a split second, we were inside a translucent cabin, looking out at a forest of dazzling lightning bugs and trees with bright red leaves.

"We're here," the hummingbird said simply.

"And so are we," said a loud voice from behind us.

Suddenly, two men stepped out from behind a tall lattice divider. I recognized one of them, and my stomach tightened. Cilantra's killers were staring at us, not perplexed at all that they were outnumbered. My dad stepped forward and swung at one of the men. He missed and stumbled, spilling forward into the divider. My mom pulled me back with trembling hands.

The hummingbird cooed a soft song, and the room changed to the upstairs observatory.

"The Sashima found us."